# A Candlelight Ecstasy Romance™

## SHE REFUSED TO THINK . . .

She refused to make sense of her actions. She only knew that this man ignited a torrent of hidden sensations that sent a blistering rush of heat through her body.

"I must be crazy," Griffen breathed fiercely. Brandy shook her head; her fingers silenced his words, then her hands locked tightly around his neck, anxiously pulling his wonderful warm mouth back to hers.

Griffen stopped ignoring the fever rising within him. His lips were at once hard and demanding while his hands sought to conquer every inch of silken skin.

# CANDLELIGHT ECSTASY ROMANCES™

# DESIGNING WOMAN

*Elaine Raco Chase*

*A CANDLELIGHT ECSTASY ROMANCE*™

Published by
Dell Publishing Co., Inc.
1 Dag Hammarskjold Plaza
New York, New York 10017

Dell ® TM 681510, Dell Publishing Co., Inc.
Candlelight Ecstasy Romance™ is a trademark of
Dell Publishing Co., Inc., New York, New York.

ISBN: 0-440-12091-8

Printed in the United States of America
First printing—August 1982

Dear Reader:

In response to your continued enthusiasm for Candlelight Ecstasy Romances™, we are increasing the number of new titles from four to six per month.

We are delighted to present sensuous novels set in America, depicting modern American men and women as they confront the provocative problems of modern relationships.

Throughout the history of the Candlelight line, Dell has tried to maintain a high standard of excellence, to give you the finest in reading enjoyment. That is now and will remain our most ardent ambition.

Anne Gisonny
Editor
Candlelight Romances

# CHAPTER ONE

"Would you care for more coffee, sir?"

Griffen checked the gold digital watch on his wrist then nodded; he still had forty minutes before his next business appointment.

"Is there anything else *I* can do for you?" the waitress inquired. Her voice was a low seductive purr; her hip suggestively brushed against his suit-jacketed arm.

"No, this is fine." Griffen's dark eyes shifted from the thin cigar he was lighting to the still hovering young woman.

Large limpid blue eyes dominated her attractive elfin features. Her petite figure was poured into hip-hugging, navy bell bottoms, her unbound breasts strained against the short middy-styled white top, while a French sailor's cap perched at a rakish angle on her sleek cap of blond hair. The waitress's inordinately attentive service had not gone unnoticed during Griffen's luncheon meeting.

Fingering his thick black mustache, Griffen successfully hid a twisted, cynical smile. The waitress shrugged off his cool indifference and headed back toward the kitchen, the swaying of her buttocks delivering a farewell message.

The restaurant had grown strangely quiet. Two hours ago the dining room had been overflowing with a frantic luncheon crowd. Now the tables and booths were deserted, the busboys and pertly clad waitresses had retired to the kitchen, deservedly enjoying a peaceful break that left Griffen the sole occupant of the Mariner's Wharf.

He flexed his muscular shoulders and relaxed against the comfortable red leather cushion. Griffen decided he too would enjoy this blissful calm oasis on a hectic Friday. His dark eyes surveyed the extraordinary view of Tampa Bay visible from the large dining room windows.

Gently swaying palm trees rimmed the glittering blue waters of the busy marina. Three fishing trawlers were unloading their daily catch; sailboats and pleasure cruisers of various sizes gently bobbed in basin moorings. It was a serene, tranquil picture; the perfect end to a delicious, congenial lunch.

The arched wooden door of the restaurant was abruptly pushed open. Startled, Griffen watched a tall woman burst into his quiet haven. She was visibly distracted and angry, and did not even bother to apologize when her large shoulder bag slammed into his arm as she stalked by him before sliding into the adjoining booth. The incessant drumming of her fingers against the top of the leather seat only inches from him reinforced Griffen's first impression of seething rage.

The restaurant's door was again opened, this time by a huskily built man in a blue business suit, who seemed equally furious. Griffen watched the blond man hesitate before weaving his way through the collection of unoccupied tables toward the angry woman.

Brandy Abbott was fighting an overwhelming urge to turn into a female facsimile of the Incredible Hulk! Her stony blue-gray eyes coldly raked Dennis Graham's figure as he strode purposefully toward her through the empty dining room.

"Would you kindly tell me what the hell that little temper tantrum of yours was all about?" Dennis snapped brusquely, settling his stocky frame opposite hers.

"That little temper tantrum," Brandy mimicked waspishly, "was just the tip of the iceburg. How dare you treat me like some . . . some frothy dessert you can pass around to your clients!" She blazed furiously.

"Now, listen, honey, Lewis didn't mean anything—"

"The man was all over me," Brandy interrupted harshly, "while you just sat there—grinning!"

"He's harmless."

She snorted and continued to glare at him.

Dennis shifted uncomfortably under her piercing gaze. "You could have handled it a little better," he mumbled, studying the contents of the salt shaker. "I mean stepping on his foot was a little rough."

"He's lucky that's all I decided to step on," she returned sarcastically.

"I don't know why you're making so much out of this," he persisted, reaching over to gently massage her arm.

Brandy disengaged his hand. "Don't pat me, Dennis. I am not some high-strung poodle that needs to be petted. I just can't believe the way you encouraged that disgusting insect! How would you like it if he was mauling Cynthia?"

"Let's leave my wife out of this," he ordered in a low, warning tone.

"No, I think it's time we brought her and her father into this," Brandy demanded sharply. "It's because of Cynthia I didn't get the money you promised me."

"I just knew you weren't going to let that matter rest," Dennis grated in annoyance. "It was business and you know it. I had to take her with me on that trip."

"All I know is that I'm tired of your broken promises. I'm tired of the pressure and the emotional strain. I'm tired of our little office charade so your father-in-law, Victor, won't find out who I am and what I really do."

"Now, honey, I've never seen you like this before." His hazel eyes widened expressively. "It must be your time of the month. Maybe if you took the rest of the day off . . ."

"Of all the stupid, sexist, Neanderthal remarks!" Brandy growled contemptuously. Her slender fingers closed around a gleaming silver butter knife. "Just get it through that thick head of yours, Dennis, that

12

it's over. It was hard enough keeping this secret from Victor, but now that your wife is coming into the office, the charade is over." Brandy forcefully brought the blunt knife nearer his chest. "I think it's time everything came out into the open."

"Don't nag me," Dennis cautioned, quickly rescuing the knife from her hand. He hastily put it and the rest of the silverware safely out of her reach.

"Oh, so now I'm the nag!"

"You should be grateful to me for all I've done for you."

"All you've done!" Brandy shrieked, then lowered her voice when she saw a dark head in the next booth. "Oh, thank you, magnificent one!" she cracked dryly.

"Wait a minute! You aren't doing so badly," he reminded her defensively, his fingers loosening the knot of his striped tie. "I've been very generous with you."

"Generous!" Brandy's jaw dropped in shock. "Dennis, you're the only one who's benefiting, and you damn well know it."

"It seems to me you were mighty anxious when we started this," he charged, raking a hand through his thick blond hair.

"I was a naive, optimistic fool," she muttered bitterly. Then her head snapped up. "But I'm no fool now. I am through being manipulated and used. For the first time I'm seeing things clearly. You're not going to use me anymore."

"Just . . . just what are you saying?" Dennis asked cautiously, not liking the quiet calm in Brandy's voice.

"I am through with this whole foolish masquerade. It's over, ended, finished."

"You . . . you can't!" Dennis jumped anxiously and grabbed her shoulders.

"Oh, yes, I can." Brandy wrenched herself free. "I don't need you anymore. I can make it on my own."

"That's what you think, honey." Dennis smiled nastily. "You think opportunity is going to drop into your lap? That what you've got with me is going to be easy to replace?"

"I can replace you just like that," Brandy challenged, snapping her fingers under his nose.

"You think so," he sneered. "Well, we'll just see how long it takes before you come crawling back. Begging me to—"

"It will be a cold day in hell before I ever come back, Dennis," she said in a low, deadly voice that marked the end of their discussion.

Dennis Graham took a deep breath and stood up. His hazel eyes studied the polished tips of his leather shoes. "Listen, can't we—"

"No, we can't," Brandy answered, staring past him to concentrate on the polished walnut walls of the restaurant.

He opened his mouth, then closed it when he saw the stony, set expression on her face. *Maybe later,* Dennis thought sullenly. Then he turned and walked out of the dining room.

Brandy Abbott continued to sit and stare. Gradually her breathing returned to normal and her pulse rate dropped. She felt a controlled calm settle over her turbulent emotions.

Movement in the adjoining booth caused her to

14

turn. Her smoky blue eyes collided and locked with the piercing brown gaze of a tall, rough-looking man.

Griffen's dark brow arched perceptively. The young woman had been nothing more than a leggy, pastel-clad blur when she ran past his table. Now that he had just heard the most intimate details of her personal life, Griffen felt compelled to examine her physical appearance.

Brown hair was pulled back by a pale pink scarf, exposing an innocent, sweetly rounded face. Her blue-gray eyes were wide and suspiciously moist. Her nose was short and straight and her full mouth devoid of any lip color. The pink and plum pansy-strewn dress, with its delicate ecru lace collar, only enhanced an image of classical purity.

Brandy caught her breath at the stranger's insolent appraisal and deliberately turned her head. Her mind registered a mental picture of tough, ruggedly carved, masculine features, deeply bronzed by the sun, with almost black hair and a rather forbidding mustache.

The man was totally unfamiliar to her and Brandy resented his willful scrutiny. When she turned hostile eyes back, the stranger had disappeared.

Well, she thought archly, it was a damn good thing he hadn't opened his mouth. She had just about had it with the entire male population!

Brandy's absorbed study of the linen weave in the red placemat ended when a tall glass filled with ice and clear liquid was literally pushed under her nose.

"From the look on your face, this is one time I think you could use a drink."

She looked up at the slim, dark-haired man stand-

15

ing next to her and smiled ruefully into his teasing gray eyes. "I think you might be right," she agreed and picked up the frosty glass, taking a healthy swallow of gin and tonic. "I just ended things with Dennis Graham."

"Ended?"

She took a deep breath, ten nerveless fingers gripped the beverage glass for security as the enormity of her situation just hit her. "Tony, your sister has just quit her job. She has joined the ever-growing ranks of the unemployed!"

Tony Cameron rubbed a large hand over his face and frowned. "What the hell happened? You only have eight months to go before you take your architect's license exam. I thought you were going to stick it out with Keller and Graham."

Brandy turned toward him, her eyes now dull and bleak. "You know I want to be an architect more than anything else. But I . . . I just can't take the nonsense that goes on in that firm another minute."

Tony nodded sympathetically and settled his slight frame on the leather seat. "I thought you were going to talk to Dennis and get things straightened out."

"Well," she mumbled, averting her eyes from his keen gaze, "I got angry and blew up and quit."

"That's not unusual for you." Tony chuckled, patting her shoulder. "Tell big brother what happened."

She exhaled slowly and gave a humorless laugh. "I got tired of being used." Brandy quickly held up her palm, stopping his interruption. "Please don't say I told you so."

Her brother merely grinned and reached into his

shirt pocket for a cigarette. "I warned you about taking that job with Keller and Graham. Their firm goes through architects and designers faster than my customers eat peanuts at the bar."

"Well, my initial deal with Dennis had such great possibilities," she returned glumly. "I was to go in as their interior designer and work with the architects. But Victor Keller is impossible!" Brandy announced angrily. "For a man who supposedly retired and turned his business over to his son-in-law, Keller comes in every day and annoys everyone with the most idiotic suggestions.

"After he leaves, Dennis troops in and contradicts all of Victor's orders. Today Cynthia showed up and demanded that I help her redecorate her house, all for free of course."

"Of course," Tony repeated lightly, his eyes watching the narrow curl of smoke disappear courtesy of the air-conditioning system. "They are users, Brandy, you'll find them in any profession and it's a damn shame such a group was your first encounter."

"I loved working with the architects. I was learning so much more than I had in college." She sighed woefully, resting her cheek in her palm.

"It's a shame you couldn't have managed to hang on just a little longer."

Brandy shrugged, her white teeth gnawing her lower lip reflectively. "If I didn't have such an explosive temper . . ." her voice trailed off. Why was it a person thought of alternatives to anger after the rage subsided?

"You could always go back," Tony pointed out logically.

She straightened her back, her chin jutting out defensively. "It gets to be a matter of principle," Brandy said roughly. "Dennis promised that the firm would reimburse me for the solar energy seminar I attended, but then he had to take Cynthia with him on a business trip, so my refund was canceled. He also promised to tell Victor just how much of the design work I've been doing on the industrial complex project, especially since the senior architect quit three weeks ago, leaving me the only one who worked on it from its inception. Dennis reneged on that and my raise."

"I can't believe Keller didn't know you were doing so much," Tony mused thoughtfully, stubbing out his cigarette.

"Well, that was my fault," his sister grumbled uncomfortably. "I agreed to do the work at home. Dennis told Victor he had hired a free-lancer named B. Jabbott."

"You ran your middle initial in with your last name and created another person?" he accused sharply, staring at her in disbelief.

Brandy nodded, her face tinged pink with embarrassment. "Oh, I know it's totally opposite to all my outspoken principles, Tony, but Dennis promised to come through with a permanent job once I passed my license exam. Do you know how hard it is for a woman to make it as an architect?"

"At least Graham recognizes talent when he sees it," her brother conceded brusquely. "Look what you did to this place. When I first bought the Wharf, it was nothing but a dilapidated bar with a seedy reputation and a great location. You gutted the in-

18

terior and redesigned and decorated it into one of Tampa's most talked about and most popular restaurants."

Brandy smiled gratefully at his compliments. Her luminous gaze shifted lovingly to roam over the interior of the dining room.

Mariner's Wharf had been created in the image of a plush dining saloon on an eighteenth-century schooner. The carpeting and upholstered Georgian furnishings were in rich tones of red and gold. Geometric carved walnut panels with polished brass railings shimmered on the walls; the beamed, coffered ceilings and carved pilasters gave it the arched effect of a ship's interior as did the delicate oil paintings that depicted ports of call. A wall of arched glass windows gave patrons a breathtaking view of Tampa Bay.

By day, with its perkily clad waitresses, its placemats and ironstone, the Wharf catered to the business lunch crowd. At night, the dining room gleamed with white linen, china, and crystal, its elegantly clad waiters serving the best in gourmet cuisine. At any time the feeling of sailing on a century-old brigantine enchanted the diners.

"I don't want this and a few other pet projects to be my only achievements. I love interior designing, but I love creating buildings more," Brandy told her brother earnestly. "An architect is first an artist, arranging beautiful shapes and forms into engineering masterpieces. I want to combine my imagination, business, mechanical, and design concepts into something people can use and enjoy. I don't want to be another Frank Lloyd Wright and I don't possess the genius of Buckminster Fuller. I can only walk in my own shoes, but I do have talent."

"I'm sorry things fell apart," Tony commiserated gently. "You could have started as an architect with Keller and Graham then worked at building your own business."

"With Victor Keller's attitude about women, I'm not so sure I would have been allowed to join the firm," she returned angrily. "He doesn't believe women should vote, let alone design buildings. Barefoot and pregnant is his motto. I vowed my first building assignment would be to fit him into a concrete sarcophagus!"

Brandy leaned forward, tapping her index finger on the wooden table. "I get fed up with all the platitudes you men keep handing out. You've been intimidating the entire female population since its puberty!"

"Now wait just a minute!" Tony jumped in defensively.

"It's an age old story, brother," Brandy continued, her voice overruling any objections. "When girls first begin to bud, they are subjected to the crudest playground jokes. If they show any signs of intelligence they're eggheads. If they don't come across in the back seat of a car for the high school football hero, they're abnormal.

"In college if you are reasonably attractive and get good grades, then you're accused of playing slap-and-tickle with your professors. When you get into the business world, the male executive views every female with a thirty-eight-inch bust as having a complete lobotomy.

"Lord help you if you do show signs of being creative and ambitious. Then they say you are aggressive and pushy. If you start getting any recognition, the office vipers have you bedding every male from the janitor on up. It's chauvinistic hostility that assumes women can get to the top only on their backs."

Tony blinked, then threw back his head and laughed. "I knew you were a fighter the day Mom brought you home from the hospital. I thought it was the end of the earth when she remarried and then when she got pregnant! Well, twelve-year-old boys have a hard time handling their own adolescent problems let alone news like that!"

His face softened into a smile. "Then you arrived. A chubby cantankerous bundle that I got stuck babysitting." Tony reached out and took his sister's hand. His long fingers twisted the gold zodiac signet ring he had given her on her last birthday. "You are a true Scorpio, Brandy. A fighter of outworn ideas and attitudes, persistent and fierce of pride."

She laughed and captured his hands in a loving grasp. "It takes one to know one, brother, especially the fierce pride part," she added subtly.

Tony cleared his throat, his right brow raising accusingly. "I get the feeling a lecture is coming."

"You're right," she bantered lightly but her hazy eyes were very serious. "I talked to Rita last night."

"Leave it alone, Brandy," Tony cautioned, moving to slide out of the banquette seat.

She gripped his hands with such force it surprised them both. "If you're not careful, this trial separation is going to end up in a divorce. I love you, Tony, but you are a stubborn, proud Scorpio yourself. You and Rita have to start talking."

"If I wanted a marriage counselor, I'd call a professional," he muttered uncomfortably.

"That's not a bad idea," Brandy agreed gently, releasing his hands to smile at him. "If you two could just get together. Rita seemed anxious to talk."

He sighed, raking agitated fingers through his dark hair. "How is she? Did she . . . did she ask about me?"

"She did. I told her the truth, Tony," she told her brother bluntly. "That you've lost twenty pounds in the last month and a half, the gray in your hair is beginning to outnumber the brown, and you look more like fifty than forty."

Tony grunted, averting his eyes to look out the window at a passing sailboat headed out to the Gulf. "How is Rita?"

"She sounds lonely, scared and—" Brandy hesitated, catching her lower lip for a second before continuing "—she isn't feeling well. She has a doctor's appointment today."

Tony's head snapped around, his gray eyes watching his sister's face with burning intensity. "Is it serious?"

Brandy shrugged. "I don't know." Her fingers toyed with the bobbing ice cubes in her drink. "You could always drive to Ft. Meyers and find out," she suggested evenly.

"Oh, I get it," he accused sarcastically. "This is a little plot you cooked up to make me worry."

"I would never do such a thing!" Brandy retorted heatedly. "But it wouldn't hurt—"

"Look, I know you're trying to be helpful, but there are things you don't understand and, frankly, are none of your business."

She gave an unladylike snort, then smiled. "I'm not in any position to argue that point. My own personal life is nothing to draw on for inspiration these days." Brandy exhaled a long sigh. "I may be a feminist, but that doesn't mean I wear combat boots and only date my own sex."

"Maybe you could make some adjustments in your own image," her brother countered amiably, reaching for another cigarette.

She frowned. "I suppose I could. But it would be a false image. I am not the delicate, clinging, whimpering type. Why can't I be me? Why can't the system accept me?"

"System?" he blinked. "What system?"

"The system!" she retorted sharply. "Having the commissioner of police as a father was extremely socially deterring. All my dates were afraid they'd be grilled and frisked; they never laid a hand on me." She shook her head sadly.

"Then I had to develop a penchant for mechanical drawing, math, and engineering—all traditionally male courses. I'm sure my assertive, aggressive personality doesn't help," Brandy admitted, her lips twisting in self-condemnation.

"All the men I meet run scared and feel emasculated. Then they turn it around so that I'm the one who is abnormal . . . frigid. Men like amiable, pliable women. Even television attempts to cut the real, live independent woman down to size by making her into the wicked, castrating bitch just to soothe the male

23

audience who might feel threatened. Men have this great philosophy—that women are wonderful and every man should own one."

"Own? Don't you think that's a little strong?" Tony chided.

Brandy shook her head. "No. You don't see it. You're in a contained environment here at the restaurant. But I went through five years of college, studying in a predominantly male field and was, unfortunately for my social life, too damn good at it. On the construction sites I'm the one giving orders and ordering the materials. I dampen egos and it's not intentional."

Tony scratched his cheek reflectively. "I remember being unusually nervous when I first met Rita two years ago," he admitted. "I had checked around and found her advertising agency was the best. She had a reputation for being a dynamo and a shrewd business woman. But the more we worked together on a campaign for the restaurant, the quicker my fears disappeared. We relaxed with each other and became good friends . . ." His voice trailed off; his gray eyes looked desolate.

"Well," Brandy sighed wistfully, resting her chin in her palm, "maybe when I find a new job I'll meet someone who'll understand just how important my career is to me. "First—" she wrinkled her nose "—I've got to get that job."

Tony refocused his gaze on his sister's smiling face. He stubbed out his cigarette, then reached into the back pocket of his slacks. "I wasn't going to show this to you. I know you wanted to do more architectural design projects rather than interior decorating.

24

But since you are gainfully unemployed, you might be interested." He handed her a five-by-eight-inch elegantly printed brochure.

Brandy opened the pristine white cover, eyeing the engraved copy with interest. "Triton Shoals?"

"It's a new private residential community being built on the north peninsula of Daytona Beach," Tony explained. "An old army buddy of mine is the developer. He's here looking for more innovative architects, designers, and contractors for phase two of the project."

"Why does he need an interior decorator?"

"Phase one, a fifty-unit condominium will be finished in another six weeks. Thirty-five of the fifty units are under sales contracts. He wants a professional decorator to set up the four different models for future sales and to be available to help the new owners. Notice the price tag on those units?"

One delicate brow arched. "For this six-figure price, they should get an entire design school."

Tony laughed. "This is ocean front with the best of everything. The north peninsula is one of the hottest spots in the state."

"There are a lot of good decorators in Daytona," Brandy pointed out logically.

"Well, apparently he hasn't found one he likes and can work with," her brother remarked. "He was very impressed with the before-and-after photos of the restaurant and my old apartment over the office."

"Oh, Tony," she groaned in disgust, pushing the pamphlet across the table, "what else was the poor man to say when you told him your little sister did it."

25

"I didn't say you were my sister; I know how you are about getting any help," he returned on the defensive. "I said a friend, B. J. Abbott, structurally redesigned and decorated both places. I also showed him the five-page spread you had in that decorating magazine last month and the blueprints for the solar energy house you designed for Mom and your dad in Palm Beach."

Brandy pulled the brochure open again. "Is this all the information you have on Triton Shoals?" She tried to sound casual but failed.

"No. I've got quite a collection of brochures, floor plans, a prospectus, and the like. Actually," Tony confided eagerly, "I'm thinking of investing in one of the condos."

Brandy flipped the booklet over. "G. St. Clair, St. Clair Development Company," she read aloud.

Tony smiled. "We nicknamed him The Saint in 'Nam. He seemed to have an invisible halo over him all during combat. He pulled more wounded men to safety and was decorated more times than any guy in our outfit. He was a hero in a war that honored no heros, only to come home to find his wife had been entertaining a large segment of the civilian male population," he added on a bitter note.

Brandy winced. "I take it he's now divorced."

Her brother nodded. "He moved from San Francisco to Daytona last year. His father owned a land developing company and when he died, The Saint took it over."

Brandy drummed her fingers on the table; her smooth forehead puckered. "Tony, when you said he was interested in more unique ideas for phase two of Triton Shoals, what exactly did you mean?"

"Well, from what I understand, he doesn't want another run-of-the-mill condo community. Phase one was already set up and started by his father, but he wants something totally different on the rest of the land. He's open for suggestions."

Her eyes lit up with excitement. "I have this project I did in college that might interest him. Do you think he'd look at a presentation from an almost-architect, especially if it's a woman?"

"Listen, St. Clair doesn't have a prejudicial bone in his body. Get your stuff together; he's staying at the Marriott. I'll call him and—"

"No!" Brandy jumped in quickly. "I want to get this on my own. Please, Tony. There's no way he'll know I'm your sister unless you tell him. Our last names are different, we don't resemble each other, and all I ever use is my initials on my work. I'll call and tell him that you mentioned the decorating assignment. Then I'll see if he'd be interested in seeing my other project."

"If that's the way you want it." Tony shrugged. "I think you're crazy. You're damn good and a little nepotism never hurt."

She shook her head. "I'll continue to be B. J. Abbott, A.S.I.D. If anything does come out of this, it will be on my own merit."

"Okay." Tony laughed and squeezed Brandy's hand. "I'll let you handle it any way you want. The rest of the brochures are in my office. Say, I didn't even ask if you had lunch?"

"Suddenly I'm very hungry." She grinned. They

both slid out of the booth and wandered toward the kitchen.

"Hey, Tony!" It was Mike Harris, the bartender, whose voice halted their progress. "Helen called. Her little boy came down with chicken pox and she won't be in tonight."

"Great!" Tony moaned. His eyes widened as he looked at his sister. "Say, Brandy, could you do me a big favor tonight?"

"Sure."

"I've got a restaurant owner's meeting, so I can't sub for Helen and we're into our vacation schedules. Do you think you could play hostess all night? You've done it before."

"No problem." She smiled. "Lately my Friday nights as well as my weekends have been very free."

"Well, you'll be very busy tonight," he told her quickly. "Do me one little favor." Tony reached over and untied the pink scarf that held back her hair. His fingers fluffed out a mass of silky amber-gold waves that fell in a tumble to her shoulders. "Wear your hair loose, throw on one of those breath-holding dresses you designed, put on some more makeup, and you'll dazzle the customers."

"I was just complaining about being served as a dessert for one of Dennis Graham's clients; now you want to turn me into an hors d'oeuvre for the Wharf's supper crowd!" Brandy teased with mock huffiness.

"Listen, I'm in the restaurant business to make money, and I know just what an appealing little appetizer my sister can be when she tries."

"Don't worry." Brandy laughed. "I promise I

28

won't disgrace you or your establishment. But it's going to cost you dinner too."

"Who knows?" Tony smiled, his eyes glinting devilishly as he held open the kitchen door. "Maybe you can find an interesting entree for yourself."

## CHAPTER TWO

The antique white mirror reflected three images: a gold Princess telephone, a brochure of a condominium, and the shower-damp, disconcerted features of Brandy Jerome Abbott.

Two elbows jockeyed for a position among the cosmetics and the pamphlets that littered the dressing table. Brandy cupped her face in the palms of her hands and stared into the mirror, smoky blue eyes silently pleading for direction staring back while her lips twisted in rueful wisdom.

This morning the bedroom mirror had shown an interior designer with eight months of internship to complete before taking the architect's licensing exam; this afternoon that same mirror reflected an unemployed woman.

Brandy grimaced at her likeness; while she was no longer employed by the architectural firm of Keller and Graham, she was in little financial danger. She still had her affiliation with one of the major furniture showrooms on Florida's Gulf coast as an interior decorator and had recently signed a lucrative contract with a national handyman's magazine to design building plans for do-it-yourself home carpenters. Yet neither of these projects gave her the pleasure that architecture did.

Brandy pushed herself away from the dressing table, dragged her feet through the buttercup shag carpeting, then dropped facedown on the lavish floral-patterned bedspread. She rolled over, ignoring the uncomfortable bunching of her terry shower wrap to stare in thoughtful contemplation at the diplomas that adorned the apple-green bedroom walls.

The last nine years of her life had been devoted to one goal—architecture. There were sixty thousand licensed architects in the United States and only a small number of them were women. Brandy had always known her target. She was determined to swell the female ranks by one and accomplish that feat by the end of this year.

At times she could literally taste her license. She had worked her way through trade school and college, collecting degrees in interior decorating and design, fashion design, a bachelor's degree in architecture with two years advance study in that field. Last June she had garnered the second highest mark on the design test and now all that was left was the four-part licensing exam in December.

Brandy closed her eyes and smiled, remembering all the free-lance decorating and fashion design assignments she had taken to support herself and her prolonged studies. Not only had she sacrificed her personal life for her chosen career, but she had taken considerable harassment from male students and professors as well.

Brandy had gone through life with three handicaps—her height, her I.Q. and her looks. She could do little to change any of them.

She excelled in all fields of mathematics, physics, and art. During high school she had managed to invade the industrial arts class and accomplished its curriculum as easily as she had managed home economics.

Her height proved to be as formidable as her I.Q. Brandy hit puberty and the seventy-inch mark by the age of thirteen. It left her shy and awkward, a condition that kept perpetuating itself as her body began to develop in other dimensions as well. Advanced studies kept Brandy occupied and strict parents kept her ignorant of the fact that her Junoesque proportions were aesthetically pleasing to the male population.

Brandy was more earthy than beautiful. Her eyes drifted between a smoky haze and a sea blue; her thick hair was not brown, not blond, not auburn, but a blend like the liquor that echoed her name. Despite her twenty-seven years, the contours of her face had not turned angular but stayed youthfully round and subtly sensual on top of her centerfold body.

It was that image that plagued her college years and made it difficult for her to get jobs. When men did finally venture to look above her well-rounded curves, they found it difficult to believe her head was filled with more than air.

Brandy had become adept at dodging playful pats

on the posterior and handling sexual innuendos that sounded like jokes. It was an exercise in degradation that spurred her on to a cynical misandry. She cultivated a cool, aggressive personality that left her a lot of time to pursue her architectural studies.

It was that same self-willed, tenacious, and determined attitude that made the men she did work with overlook her measurements and respect her talent and competence.

Brandy's narrowed gaze focused on the bright orange fiberglass hardhat that winked in the late afternoon sunlight on the wicker bookcase. The hat had been a gift from the construction crew that had worked on Mariner's Wharf. It was no mere decoration but a symbol of her professional ability.

Tony's restaurant had been her baby from birth and she had proved to be an exceptional mother. After completing her remodeling designs, Brandy hired the best structural engineers and contractors she could find as well as the most artistic finishers.

When the construction manager realized he was dealing with the boss and not a secretary, Brandy experienced the same type of reaction she had always received—astonishment. But as the job progressed and she worked side-by-side with the crew, their chauvinistic, patronizing attitudes began to disappear.

Brandy was an old-fashioned architect. She didn't design by computer but by hand, researching and checking all the specifications and materials right down to the weight capacity of the bolts used in framing. She was first and foremost her client's principal and trusted agent. She dealt directly with all the subcontractors and allowed no fast-tracking or cost-cutting.

Brandy had vowed early in her career that she would never save cents to lose lives in some needless and preventable construction accident. It was an attitude that earned her respect from the men she worked with and praise that harbored no sexual stereotyping.

She wanted very badly to put her talents to work again. Her mind wandered back to the Tritan Shoals condominium complex. It was a ten-story, fifty-unit highrise that offered discerning owners a luxurious home overlooking sea boats, coquina rock, sand dunes, and the awe-inspiring Atlantic Ocean.

Brandy scrambled off the bed and crossed to the dressing table. She looked down at the brochures, pamphlets, and prospectus that contained all the pertinent information on the project. Tritan Shoals was the epitome of security, safety, and privacy. It featured underground parking, a closed-circuit TV, a security patrol, the latest in fire protection, and the advantage of secluded, staggered balconies.

Artistically and architecturally the design of the condo was typical of the concrete elegance that freckled most of the Florida coast. Tritan Shoals was an exclusive community that provided such amenities as a heated swimming pool, separate exercise and sauna rooms, a large social room, tennis courts, putting green, plus a private marina and docking facilities.

The interior floor plans showed spacious one-, two-, and three-bedroom units and five custom-designed penthouses. Each residence commanded a panoramic view of the ocean as well as of the Halifax River from the private balconies. Every known modern appliance was built into the kitchen. The master bathroom sported a thermal whirlpool as well as other luxurious appointments.

Brandy's decorating talents had touched many a condo on the Gulf Coast, but none were comparable to the sumptuous environment extolled by the brochures of Tritan Shoals. However elegant, it would still be a challenge to turn a myriad of rough white plaster walls into a unique yet livable home. Perhaps an even greater challenge awaited her if she could get Mr. G. St. Clair interested in her architectural project for phase two of his development.

Brandy nervously wiped her lips against the back of her hand and stared at the telephone number of the Marriott that she had scribbled on the back of one of the pamphlets. She took a deep breath, lifted the receiver and let her index finger punch her into a realm of new and exciting possibilities.

The telephone was on its seventh ring and Brandy was just about to hang up when a very irritated, very impatient voice growled "St. Clair" in her ear.

Her stomach plunged, making her sound nervous and contrite. "Mr . . . Mr. St. Clair." She quickly gulped in air. "This is B. J. Abbott. Tony Cameron suggested I get in touch with you about your Tritan Shoals complex."

"Tony?" The word came out gruff and annoyed. There was a long pause.

Brandy fidgeted uncomfortably and the phone cord became wrapped around her arm. This was one hell of a way to make an impression on a new business acquaintance!

"You're the decorator who did such a great job on Tony's restaurant."

"Yes, I did. I mean I am. I . . ." She was babbling like an adolescent. She cleared her throat, her hand tightening on the receiver as if to absorb some magical strength. "Mr. St. Clair, I wanted to discuss the design project. Am I catching you at an inconvenient time?"

Complete silence. Brandy closed her eyes and groped her way into the boudoir chair. Apparently this was not going to be her day to win friends and influence people.

A very masculine, very deep, very amused chuckle snaked through the line into her ear and vibrated warmly down her spine. "Miss Abbott, I do apologize. I am standing here dripping wet, trying to juggle one of those impossibly small hotel towels and the telephone."

"I'm . . . I'm sorry," Brandy stammered, feeling her cheeks suffuse with color. "Why don't I call you later? Why don't you call me?"

"Why don't—" he interrupted in a calm voice "—you give me a minute to rewrap my towel, get a cigar, and pull up a chair. I would like to talk to you."

Brandy felt slightly more reassured by his congenial tone. She couldn't understand why she was reacting so out of character. She was a professional who had dealt with numerous personalities, and here she was stuttering like an amateur. Even her usually well-modulated voice sounded oddly high, and she had to control herself from speaking too quickly.

"Now, Miss Abbott." The deep voice was back on the line, pleasant and amiable. "I assume you've already digested the prospectus and the brochures I gave Tony." At her affirmative answer he continued. "Why don't you listen to the speech I've been reciting all day and then you can ask any questions I don't answer.

"The decorating assignment is by contract with an additional commission. There are three models to be set up, plus one penthouse for my personal use. The condo will be ready in six weeks. I realize that's not much time.

"You'll be your own boss; you can hire additional help; no one will second-guess you. Money is no object.

"Some of the absentee owners will undoubtedly request your services as, I imagine, will other residents. Those arrangements will be left entirely up to you." He paused.

"I was very impressed with the work you've done for Tony. I happened into the Hampton Bank Building today, and when I inquired about the designer of their lobby, the name B. J. Abbott once again surfaced." The voice lowered persuasively. "I hope you've become interested in Tritan Shoals."

"You are very complimentary, Mr. St. Clair," Brandy acknowledged, a smile in her voice. "I am interested in the Shoals. I won't take up your valuable time by listing my accreditations. My portfolio, credentials, contacts, and references speak for themselves. I will tell you that I have done interiors in quite a number of the condos along the Pinellas Sun-coast."

"Have you done any work along the Atlantic Coast?"

"No, no, I haven't. I had quite a few contracts on the Gulf and some family here," Brandy told him. She didn't mention that she was born in Palm Beach and her reluctance to go back and work there was due to her parents' considerable connections. After graduation, she wanted to make a name for herself without wondering if being Brandon Abbott's, the police commissioner's daughter, made her clients feel intimidated.

"Well, I'm a transplanted Californian," the rough voice announced, "and I've never regretted the move. Daytona has so much to offer. Its location is very conducive to business. Volusia County is one of the strongest growth areas in the country and pros-perous compared to other towns in Florida. It shows a good, steady development despite the highly vola-tile interest rates.

"There's a vast world of entertainment in Dayto-na, not only golf, tennis, and the ocean, but Grey-hound racing, jai alai and, of course, the Speedway." He stopped and laughed self-consciously. "I must sound like the Chamber of Commerce."

"No, you sound like a man who is very content." Brandy took a deep breath. "Mr. St. Clair, I am interested in learning about phase two of the Tritan Shoals project. I read the notations on the prospectus and saw your rough sketch of the land."

"Phase two?" He sounded puzzled. "So far that's a twenty-five acre, L-shaped peninsula that was just reclaimed from a mangrove- and palm-treed swamp filled with snakes and mosquitos. It is, however, a beautiful piece of property."

Brandy had to smile at the obvious warmth in Mr. St. Clair's voice as he continued. "It's surrounded on three sides by the Atlantic with a buffer of coquina rock. Whatever is built, the beach will be protected. I want the dunes to be preserved against trampling and erosion. This will be the first time I've handled a project right from conception. I still haven't found the right thing . . ." His voice trailed off.

"But you'd like it to be something more than the concrete and steel pyramids that are now lining the coast."

He laughed, a low rich sound that caused an electrical impulse to jolt Brandy's system. "Very nicely put, Miss Abbott. I would indeed like more. Can you suggest an architect?"

"Me."

Suddenly Brandy knew the definitive meaning of the phrase "pregnant pause." But then she had heard the sound of astonished silence before. "Mr. St. Clair —" her tone was soothing and her words seeped in patience "—I realize I'm a late arrival on the Shoals project. I do happen to have plans for a unique, luxurious, and expensive housing complex and, to be perfectly blunt, you have the perfect parcel of land and the financial backing."

"What firm are you with?"

Brandy smiled slightly. "As of this afternoon I am unemployed."

"I see."

"No, you don't." This was no time for half-truths;

39

she plunged confidently ahead. "I severed my internship with a local firm that mainly designed industrial warehouses. I have no objection to hard work, in fact that's how I've gotten my degrees, but I have been putting in the proverbial forty-hour days for the last ten months. There were also a lot of internal office management problems and they had difficulty believing a woman could design more than domestic space."

"And can you design more than domestic space, Miss Abbott?" St. Clair asked evenly.

"I'll let you be the judge of that."

He laughed. "I like you, Miss Abbott. You're aggressive, enthusiastic, and honest."

"Those are words I don't often hear, Mr. St. Clair," Brandy told him with obvious pleasure.

"I'd be interested in looking at your housing plans." His voice grew serious. "I am certainly not going to veto it just because you're a woman. After all, William Randolph Hearst selected Julia Morgan to design San Simeon."

"I won't be giving you anything *that* lavish," she returned lightly. "But I am pleased with your attitude. There are a great many pressures and hardships for women in this career, with sexual discrimination heading the list especially if you are reasonably attractive."

"And are you, Miss Abbott?" He sounded intrigued.

Brandy's gaze snagged the image reflected in her dressing table mirror. Despite the damp hair and soap-scrubbed face, her cheeks were tinged with more color than any blusher could manufacture and her eyes glittered like jewels.

She heard him chuckle at her lengthy silence. "Perhaps I should invest in videophones; then I could see for myself," St. Clair teased.

"You'd find we were similarly attired in scanty towels," Brandy responded impishly, watching not only her face but her entire body take on a rosy glow.

"I wish I had this evening free, Miss Abbott," St. Clair countered regrettably. "Unfortunately I have a previous dinner engagement with an old family friend."

"I'm afraid I too am similiarly occupied." Brandy was surprised at how disappointed she sounded. "When will I be able to meet you?"

"I'm here until Wednesday and am heavily booked with pre-arranged appointments."

Brandy gnawed her lower lip thoughtfully. "My portfolio needs minor updating and the architectural project will need a little finishing as well. I could bring them by your hotel on Sunday."

"Fine. That will give me time to look them over." St. Clair cleared his throat. "Keep in touch by phone if you have any other questions. I do have another engagement on Sunday, but I'll try to arrange it so I can be free to have dinner with you."

"I'd like that," Brandy said warmly. "I really appreciate all the time you've given me."

"My pleasure, Miss Abbott." St. Clair paused. "If I don't manage to break away on Sunday, leave your presentation with the desk clerk. I do intend to see you," he warned sternly. "Good evening."

The hum of the dial tone serenaded Brandy for a

41

full minute before she realized the connection had been broken. Why couldn't more men have St. Clair's open attitude? He was so receptive, so interested and so complimentary—no cavalier attitude here!

He also had one of the nicest laughs and quite possibly the most sensual and deepest voice she had ever heard. Brandy cursed the fact that Southern Bell had not gone to videophones. She was anxious to see whether St. Clair's physical attributes harmonized with his vocal ones.

Brandy eyed the digital display on her alarm clock and hastily decided her physical attributes needed to be harmonized and synchronized. After all, she was to be the apéritif to the patrons at Mariner's Wharf this evening.

The restaurant had been overbooked. Customers with reservations had a thirty-minute wait, without reservations almost two hours in which to enjoy the musical trio and the exotic specialty drinks that were served in the Porthole Lounge. In addition to her duties as hostess, Brandy helped the busy waiters by taking pre-dinner cocktail orders and made sure the busboys paid prompt attention to cleaning the tables for the next sitting.

Tall and regal, Brandy stood in the archway that connected the main dining room to the bar. A soft smile curved her lips. Despite the rush of customers and the persistently ringing telephone, the evening was progressing smoothly. There were no problems to plague Tony when he returned from his restaurant owner's meeting and Brandy had to admit she was enjoying her role of mistress of all she surveyed.

The broad shoulders and back of a male customer waiting patiently at the hostess's station snagged Brandy's attention. She quickly weaved around the fully occupied tables, nodding and exchanging pleasantries with the diners while keeping one eye on the back of an impeccably tailored gray suit.

"Welcome to Mariner's Wharf." She greeted the man in a breathless, husky voice, as she slid quietly into her station.

The man turned and Brandy's smoky blue gaze collided with a pair of dark brown eyes. Her forehead puckered in thoughtful contemplation; her welcoming smile faded ever so slightly. She had the distinct impression she should know this rugged-looking, black mustachioed face.

Griffen arched a dark brow. Wasn't this the same woman who had occupied the booth adjoining his in this very restaurant just six hours ago? His narrowed, cynical eyes inspected her deliberately.

Gone was the well-scrubbed innocent face and childish ponytail. In its place were pastel shadowed, diamond-bright eyes, inviting mauve-tinted lips and side-parted, flowing hair that shimmered with liquid gold and sable highlights.

She was taller than he'd imagined and surprised that her head was almost on his eye level considering his own six-foot-three frame. And while this afternoon's schoolgirl dress had cleverly concealed her rounded proportions, this evening's outfit was guaranteed to make grown men salivate over more than gourmet cuisine. A tapered black crepe skirt encased

43

her slim hips while her full breasts were saved from exposure by a diagonal spray of silk-screened plum, blue, and silver flowers pinned onto her diaphanous black tunic top.

The man's rude examination caused Brandy to lose all vestiges of graciousness. "Do you have a reservation?" Her voice was cold and uncivil.

"I'm with the MacKenzie party," came his equally clipped response.

She consulted her seating list and noted his dinner companions had been ensconced in the large booth by the—Her mind skidded to a halt as did the hand that reached for a leatherbound menu. This man had been the occupant of the booth next to hers earlier that day! She should have recognized the rough, bronzed features and forebidding gaze sooner.

"Follow me, please," Brandy instructed with icy formality and turned to lead him through the roomful of tables. She heard his sharp intake of breath and smiled. While the front of her hostess gown caused eyebrows to rise, the rear view always elicited a gasp.

She and a friend in design school had created both the fabric and the style. The shoulder-to-waist bias spray of flowers kept the bodice of the tunic within legal limits. But the back of the dress was little more than a sheer expanse of black nylon covering Brandy's sun-toasted skin. The clingy skirt was slit to above the knee, providing freedom of movement and the visual excitement of long, sleek calves.

"I've got to admit," his low voice snarled close to her ear, "you are a fast worker. You told your friend Dennis that he could be replaced and with the bait

44

you're wearing it won't take long for some sucker to bite."

It took considerable effort, but Brandy's silver-sandaled feet never faltered and her face never lost its smile. Outwardly she remained composed; inwardly she wanted to turn and connect her fist with his square jaw. She hadn't the faintest idea why this man was making such innuendos about her character but decided the best course was one of silence.

"I'd love to know how you managed to get this job," the mocking voice continued. "Of course tears and practiced innocence work on some men but we both know you're a—"

Suddenly Brandy stopped next to a red leather banquette. She turned and let her shoulder slam against him. "Your party." Her eyes were wide and guileless.

"Griffen!" A ruddy-faced, balding man in his fifties jumped up and extended his hand.

"Sorry to be late, Mac." Griffen clasped the older man's outstretched hand and returned his smile. "I had trouble with the car I rented."

Mac made a dismissing gesture. "We just got seated ourselves. You remember my wife, Rose, and this is our daughter, Missy."

Brandy's mouth curved slightly, noting Griffen's greeting of the plump, gray-haired Rose and his obvious reluctance at occupying the vacant seat next to the pubescent, giggling Missy.

"What will you drink?" Mac inquired, anxious to play the perfect host.

Griffen leveled a dark gaze at Brandy's hovering figure. "Scotch on the rocks," he said.

She nodded and moved toward the lounge, supremely conscious of a pair of brown eyes that bore into her retreating figure like twin lasers.

Brandy slid into an unobtrusive corner of the circular bar and gave Mike Harris the drink order. She perversely decided to wait and serve Griffen herself. His caustic insinuations still grated in her ears. He had obviously listened to her conversation with Dennis, but she couldn't understand why he chose to make such cruel and misdirected comments.

Brandy leaned against the bar, her skin enjoying the soothing coolness of the brass rail through the gossamer material of her dress. She forced herself to recall the gist of her argument with Dennis. They had quarreled over money, broken promises, his wife, and her office masquerade—then she had quit.

Her eyes widened perceptively. Brandy swallowed, then choked on her own saliva. To an eavesdropper their conversation would have appeared to be the end of an affair, not the termination of employment!

Her palm slammed against the bar, making a dish of peanuts bounce in protest. That's what Griffen had thought he'd heard! A virtual stranger had sat listening to fragmented pieces of her life and then had condemned her. He had pieced together his own erotic fantasy with her as the star!

Brandy's long fingers drummed an angry rhythm against the brass railing. The absolute nerve of that man! She visualized the object of her anger. She could see the carved features of his face and the cruel twisting of his well-shaped mouth.

How dare he think he was superior enough to be

46

prosecuter, judge, and jury to a woman he didn't even know! She had half a mind to go out there and tell him. No! Why should she even dignify his allegations with an explanation? She owed him nothing.

Brandy tried to shake off her incessant rage, but it was a lesson in futility. She needed an outlet for the adrenaline seething through her system. Griffen needed to be made an example of!

Slowly a very satanic grin spread over Brandy's attractive features. Why not have a little fun? As long as he had branded her a vixen, why not continue and embellish his fantasy? She was playing hostess for one night, and he was a transient visitor she'd never see again.

Laughter bubbled low in her throat, her eyes sparkled with a life of their own. She eagerly took the Scotch from the bartender and anxiously headed back into the dining room.

Brandy viewed her quarry with amused, half-hooded eyes. Griffen was doing his best to pay attention to his host's young daughter. Missy looked barely out of her teens, with limpet blue eyes and an Alice-in-Wonderland hair style that sent long strands of corn-colored locks swishing against Griffen's expertly tailored gray suit.

For a brief moment Brandy felt her tormentor was being punished enough—then her smile broadened into a wicked grin. Why not spice up his evening a little more? Slowly and deliberately she moved toward his booth. Her self-assured carriage and long-legged, supple walk caught and held his attention. Brandy smiled at him; her brilliant eyes glittered promises of pleasure.

"Scotch on the rocks." Brandy expertly slid an embossed paper coaster and the drink between Griffen's hands. She let her thumb lightly caress his knuckles and move on to the gold digital watch at his wrist. She felt him flinch.

"Paul will be your waiter this evening," Brandy continued, her charming smile encompassing the entire group. "He'll be with you momentarily to take your orders."

She shifted her body and casually slid her right arm along the top of the leather seat. "If there is anything else you need—" her fingers surreptitiously found the collar of Griffen's pewter silk shirt and teasingly ruffled the dark coils of hair that curled at the nape of his neck "—please just let me know."

Brandy favored them with another disarming smile. At the same time, she managed to press the soft curve of her body against Griffen's arm. She turned and drifted back to the hostess's lectern, leaving the haunting scent of jasmine clinging to his suit jacket.

Being a vamp proved thrilling! Brandy had spent years disguising her inherent femininity behind a severe hair style, bland makeup, and well-tailored, figure-concealing clothes. Her businesslike, cool, and unapproachable demeanor was a necessity in her profession, if she wanted to be taken seriously.

Tonight under Griffen's disapproving eyes she felt brave and daring and reckless. The provocative dress, the heavier use of cosmetics, and the loose, wavy hair all teamed up to awaken a hidden power that had lain dormant within her. Brandy was enjoying the release of her imprisoned sexuality.

She found it very easy to make physical contact with Griffen during the evening. Every time she seated new customers, she managed to walk past his booth and some part of her anatomy touched his. Brandy enjoyed those encounters and began to look forward to the feel of Griffen's hard, muscled strength against her soft form.

She also enjoyed challenging Griffen's dark forbidding glances with coquettish flirting. The seductive fluttering of lashes and the come-hither smiles she cast in his direction only made him scowl all the more. Her coup de grâce was personally delivering complimentary after-dinner snifters of brandy to Griffen's table. Somehow it seemed fitting that he should taste the potency of her name.

An evening of continually practicing seductive wiles in addition to her restaurant duties left Brandy exhausted. Her gracious "good evening" to Griffen and the departing MacKenzie family sounded more like a sigh of relief. She did feel a pang of regret as she gazed into his virile, sun-bronzed mustachioed face for the last time.

While the Porthole Lounge was still catering to a pulsating mass of human energy, the dining room of the Mariner's Wharf had bid good-bye to the last of the evening's clientele. The chandeliers had been turned off, leaving the room to bask in the amber glow of the wall lanterns and the colorful blinking lights of the marina.

Brandy occupied the same booth she had that afternoon with Dennis. She was busy separating cash receipts from charge tickets, doublechecking the next evening's bookings, and enjoying the quiet. She paused every fifth entry to nibble one of the giant Gulf prawns she had procured from the kitchen.

"I expected to find you sinking your teeth into a more livelier fish," came a steel-edged masculine voice.

Slowly Brandy lifted her eyes from the reporting sheet and refocused them on a gray-suited, broad-shouldered figure hovering in the shadows. Nothing in her manner reflected her shock at seeing him again. "I see you easily disposed of your date." She dropped her pencil on the table and leaned back against the cool leather cushion. "It really offended me to see you waste your . . . charms . . . on a teen-ager."

"She's a sweet, innocent kid." Griffen growled, moving closer to her. "Can you claim the same?"

"She sounds boring." Brandy motioned for him to join her; she didn't like the subtle intimidation of his towering height.

Griffen slid into the opposite side of the booth. He took a hammered silver cigarette case and a matching lighter from his inside breast pocket. "I really admired you this afternoon," he told her, extracting a slim cigar from the case and placing it between his even white teeth.

Brandy's long fingers confiscated the lighter from the table and pressed the mechanical device into flame. "Admired me?" She lifted it to the end of his cigar and watched the tobacco glow in response.

Griffen looked away from her glittering diamond-bright eyes to study the blue-gray swirl of smoke. "You said you were through being manipulated and used. That you were a young, naive fool but were now seeing things more clearly." His dark gaze once again seared Brandy's face. A muscle worked ominously in his cheek. "I listened to you pull your self-respect together and end your affair. I thought you were sincere."

Brandy tilted her head thoughtfully. "But you've decided I haven't reformed." It was a statement delivered with an icy edge and a smile that never quite reached her eyes.

"It was quite obvious by your behavior tonight that you were looking for a replacement for Dennis."

"And you came all the way back here to tell me that I failed—" her eyelashes fluttered like black lace wings against her cheeks "—at least where you're concerned."

I've dealt with your kind before," Griffen returned with superior mockery. "You're nothing but a materialistic, calculating bitch who doesn't let anything stand in her way."

Materialistic! Calculating! Bitch! The arrogance of his slurs ignited the spark of battle in Brandy's soul. She had made a supreme effort in her life never to use her femininity to get ahead, and now she was being accused of functioning totally on sex. Common sense told Brandy that now was the time to set this man straight. But sense had little influence tonight.

Gracefully Brandy lifted her arms above her head and stretched, easing the anger from her tense muscles. She noted with satisfaction that Griffen's autocratic brown gaze dropped from her face to the swell of her full breasts that strained against their thin covering. "Maybe I didn't waste my efforts." Her voice was a seductive purr. "It sounds as if my kind holds a definite fascination for you."

Griffen viciously stubbed out his half-smoked cigar into a small brass ashtray. "I thought I could talk some sense into you," he growled through clenched teeth.

"Talk?" Brandy managed to look disappointed. She took another deep breath, then lowered her voice persuasively. "I talk much better in a horizontal position."

Griffen stared at her for a long moment, his mouth twisting in disgust. He pushed himself free of the booth and without a final word or backward glance, strode purposefully out of the dining room.

Brandy could feel her heart pounding against her ribs, but she was surprised to see her hands shaking. She wasn't sure whether it was suppressed anger from Griffen's allegations or the excitement of playing erotic games with a dangerously fascinating stranger. She only knew she was very glad he had left!

Brandy jumped visibly ten minutes later when another male figure loomed out of the shadows of the dining room. Her nerves returned to normal when she saw it was Tony, who had come to join her. "How was your meeting?" she inquired with a welcoming smile.

"The usual bantering back and forth. Sometimes I wonder why I even go." He shrugged his shoulders negligently. "Sorry I took so long. Did you manage all right?"

"Have you heard any complaints?" Brandy chided easily. "Everything was fine, busy as usual, and my feet are killing me." She pushed the receipts and the tally sheet toward him. "You're booked solid tomorrow too."

"Great."

Brandy frowned at her brother; he sounded anything but happy. "Tony, is something wrong?"

"Nothing for you to worry about." He smiled at her. "Come on, I'll escort your tired feet to the parking lot." Tony slid out of the booth and held out his hand.

Brandy's strong fingers curled around his in a comforting squeeze. "I didn't get a chance to tell you before you rushed off, but I called your friend St. Clair. I'm submitting a design portfolio and he's agreed to look at my architectural project."

"That's great." Tony gave his sister a proud hug. "Listen, I really appreciate your helping me tonight." He pushed open the heavy wooden front door, held it with his back, and settled both hands on Brandy's shoulders. "And if I didn't mention it before, you look sensational. Wear that dress when you see St. Clair." He grinned wolfishly at her.

"St. Clair sounds like a man who is impressed by brains rather than bodies," she countered dryly. Her prim expression suddenly softened. "Thanks for telling me about him." Brandy kissed his cheek and let her hand filter through his silver-streaked hair.

"My pleasure." Tony turned his head and looked at the jumble of cars still in the parking area. "Where's your van?"

"It's getting new brakes and shocks," Brandy told him with a wry grimace. "Marc at the repair shop loaned me that little white Chevette; it's quite a change from my van."

The distinct ringing of a telephone caught Tony's attention. Brandy saw him hesitate, then she gave him a little push back inside. "Go on, you still have bar customers. I'm parked under the light and I'm fully capable of defending myself."

"Thanks." He gave her a quick peck on the cheek and turned toward the lounge.

The lock popped easily under the influence of the silver key. A rush of hot air greeted Brandy when she opened the door of the white sub-compact. She threw her small evening purse onto the passenger's bucket seat and cranked down the window.

"I see from that interesting tableau that you've decided on your next victim."

Brandy stiffened momentarily at the sound of a voice piercing the still night air. When she realized it was the gray-suited man again, her initial fear subsided and she gave him a cool back-shoulder glance. "Hardly a victim," she countered with far more aplomb that she knew she possessed. Brandy turned and faced him. "Wasn't it you who mentioned the word 'replacement'?"

"And you've decided it's going to be your new employer?"

"Well," she drawled deliberately, "a girl has to be enterprising these days and the restaurant is very profitable and the owner is very attractive." Brandy swallowed the sour taste that formed in her mouth. She didn't like the character she was portraying, but like any good actress, she put her heart into the role.

One dark eyebrow lifted sardonically. "It seems

that I'm out of the running," was the answer Brandy received. The slanting lights and shadows of the parking lot made Griffen's granite-hard features even more forbidding.

Brandy seemed hypnotized by his magnetic gaze. She knew she was flirting with danger but somehow fear was masked by excitement. "You took yourself out of the running," she told him huskily. Her senses were sharp and alert. A torrent of strange paradoxical sensations flooded her body. She appeared cool on the surface, but inside a fever was rising, a fever she had thought had dried up but now erupted in a brilliant burning.

"Maybe I'll put myself back in." He paused, his eyes were half-hooded and unreadable. "Just to save my fellow man." His hands roughly grabbed her shoulders and he pulled her against him.

Griffen's mouth twisted cruelly over her soft lips. His kiss was relentless and punishing and a blatant display of force. But Brandy refused to succumb to his raw masculinity and began to mount a formidable defense of her own.

Her fingers easily released the two buttons on his jacket. Her hands moved slowly over his broad chest, her fingertips pressing into the firm muscles. She deliberately leaned forward and let the haughty tips of her breasts press into the thin material of his shirt. Brandy relaxed and let her pliant feminine curves mold intimately against Griffen's hard length.

Her ready compliance nudged aside his anger and let his body chemistry take over. Griffen's lips softened against hers, his tongue seeking and entering the lush interior of her mouth. His hands roamed

55

over the satiny expanse of exposed skin on her back, just as arms wrapped tightly around his waist. They were two people reveling in the heightened awareness of each other, increased by an evening of mounting sexual tension.

Sounds of laughter and voices floating on strains of music invaded their energized intimacy. Brandy pulled herself free of Griffen, hastily slid into the safety of her car, and slammed the door.

It was a shaky hand that started the ignition and engaged the gears. It took her another five minutes to realize she was driving without any headlights.

## CHAPTER THREE

Limp fingers groped along the wooden top of the night table, searching for Alexander Graham Bell's persistently ringing invention. One sleep-glued eyelid struggled open, allowing a blue-gray orb to aid in the search. The rudely screaming object-in-question was discovered miles away on the dressing table.

Grumbling dire threats to the patent office, Brandy rolled free from the snug cocoon of her bed and stumbled across the room. "Hello." The word sounded more like a moan of pain than a greeting.

"Don't tell me I woke you."

"All right, I won't . . . but you did." Her eyes were still closed. "What time is it?" The words were barely discernible through her yawn.

"Six."

"Tony, I hope for your own physical well-being that it is six P.M."

"I . . . I'm sorry." Her brother stammered his

57

apology. "I know you've only had four hours of sleep but—" He stopped and took a deep breath. "Look, I need another favor."

Brandy pushed a stray lock of hair off her cheek and ran her tongue around her teeth. She was slowly coming to life. Her brain registered the agitation in her brother's voice. "What's the favor?"

"Can you take over the restaurant for the weekend?" The words tumbled out in a rush and ran together. "I know it's a lot to ask. I know you're busy but—"

"But you've had less sleep than I've had," Brandy finished quietly, "and that's a condition you've been putting up with since your wife left."

Tony gave a humorless laugh. "You are psychic. You are also very right." He was silent for a moment. "I am going to Ft. Meyers. I am going to see Rita. I am going to get my life straightened out this weekend. I cannot live in limbo any longer." He hesitated. "Will you help?"

"Of course I'll help," she returned almost angrily. "I've been willing to help from day one! Talk about being dense, stubborn, proud, and—"

"If I wanted a lecture, I'd call our mother!" Tony interrupted roughly. "What I need is moral support."

"What you need is business support," Brandy countered dryly. "And you've got it. I will be happy to manage the Wharf this weekend."

"Mike Harris will take care of the lounge and make the late night bank deposit. I've set everything up with René in the kitchen, and Madeline will handle today's lunch crowd. You'll have dinner tonight and the Sunday crowd from four till closing."

Brandy nodded and rubbed her nose thoughtfully. "Tony, would you mind if I moved into the office apartment for the weekend? It would save me the two-hour drive and I would have more time to work on my project for St. Clair."

"Damn!" He swore angrily at his own thoughtlessness. "I forgot all about that. Brandy, listen I can get—"

"Relax," she told her brother, her voice calm and soothing, "deadlines are a way of life for me. I don't have that many changes to make and I'll be closer to the textbooks in the library."

"You are incredible." Tony breathed gratefully. "How did I ever rate such a sister?"

"Compliments are always appreciated," Brandy teased lightly, then her tone changed to one of concern. "You sound exhausted. You aren't going to try to make a three-hour drive with no sleep, are you?"

"I think I'll leave the driving to Greyhound," Tony said evenly. "That will eliminate the possibility of my temper overriding my sensibilities and turning back before I even get turned away."

"Rita will not turn you away," she said confidently. "But it will make it impossible for you to run away."

"I've stopped running," he told her. "Like you said yesterday, Rita and I have to communicate. This weekend I'll find out whether we continue together or I go it alone." There was a long pause and when he spoke again, Tony was all business. "I've left some instructions on my desk for you. If anything does come up—"

"Mike and I can handle it," Brandy returned quickly. "You take things one step at a time and, Tony, whatever you decide, I love you."

"Thanks."

Brandy stared at the phone for a long moment, then tumbled her weary body back onto the rumpled covers. Her smoky blue eyes focused on the ceiling and stared at the intricate designs visible in the early morning light.

Life resembled the whirled patterns formed in the stucco. Entangled, complex, and endless shapes that soared to sublime highs and plummeted to precipitate lows. On the inanimate ceiling it was artistic and attractive—to a person it could be heaven or it could be hell.

Heaven or hell—she had sampled both last night. Brandy rolled over and pulled a pillow under her chin. The yellow satin cover lay smooth against her face and soft against her lips. A direct contrast to the lean, stubble-roughened cheek and the mustache-lined mouth that had both attracted and assaulted her a few hours ago.

Griffen—that was the only name she knew him by. But unlike the fabled creature of Greek mythology, a mixture of keen-eyed eagle and ferocious lion, this Griffen was not the shrewd observer he surmised. This Griffen had created a favorite male fantasy and decided she was a tramp!

Yet, despite his degrading comments and his punishing kisses, Brandy found she wanted to see him again. Would he come back to the Wharf tonight?

She was anxious for another intimate battle yet terrified that he might not appear.

Brandy closed her eyes and snuggled her body into the solid bulk of the mattress. Her long fingers smoothed the pale yellow bedsheets while her mind remembered the feel of taut muscles beneath a thin silk shirt. Her face burrowed against the pillow; her nose inhaled the scent of fabric softener only to find it resembled the haunting memory of a man's cologne.

Brandy didn't know what Griffen wanted from her, but she knew what she wanted from him. Last night her head and heart were no longer synchronized. Last night glands and hormones ruled her senses.

She had never lived the life of the flesh. She had been very selective about men. Too careful, too cautious, too particular. Now she found she was totally lost in her own sensuality and completely absorbed by a stranger who thought the worst of her.

Brandy ruefully acknowledged that she had only herself to blame for perpetuating that image. She had enjoyed flirting with danger and eagerly embellished Griffen's fantasy by projecting a totally false personality. Under her erotic mask, she had to admit she felt alive and excited as never before.

Call it chemistry, call it sexual attraction, call it stupidity—Brandy knew Griffen had perceived it too. It was visible in his dark inviting eyes even if the words his lips spoke were meant to repel. If Griffen showed up tonight, Brandy had no intentions of repelling him.

Fresh juices sprang into her mouth and her face

glowed with anticipated pleasure. Brandy's night-shirt-clad figure bolted from the bed to the open louvered doors of her closet. Her fingers methodical-ly pushed aside one hanger after another until they found their target—a slim crepe dress in pale apricot. The modest cowl neckline highlighted her full breasts while the back draped low to the base of her spine. An impertinent splash of a bright orange silk rose nestled in the soft folds of material.

Blue-gray eyes studied the dress for a long time. A sour taste formed thickly on Brandy's tongue. She crushed the cool material against her fevered body. This wasn't her—or was it?

Exactly who was she? Brandy, the smoldering, sexually uninhibited lady of last night who appeared ready to trade her body in payment for a life of ease. Or was she B. J. Abbott, the cool, businesswoman whose energies revolved around her architect's li-cense and whose career meant more than her person-al life.

What type of man did she want? A rough, disdain-ful, autocrat like Griffen or . . . or a man like St. Clair. St. Clair was admittedly nothing more than a charming masculine voice on the phone, but a man who had praised her ambitious attitude, admired her aggressive manner, and was eager to see her work.

What was she doing, sitting here worrying about clothes when she had so much work to do! St. Clair was the right man—a rare man. B. J. was the right image—not the sensual Brandy. But wasn't she a combination of both?

The delicate evening dress was angrily tossed amid the twisted bedsheets. Confused by her thoughts and her emotions, Brandy stalked out of the room and headed toward her cheery yellow and white kitchen. A cup of strong coffee and a hearty breakfast would put everything in its proper perspective.

But even before the electric percolator had flashed on its red finishing light, the steam iron was warming up to press the wrinkles out of the apricot crepe.

By ten that evening the blood flowing through Brandy's veins had been replaced by caffeine. She had spent the morning updating her design portfolio and the afternoon studying structural manuals at the library. Then she had rushed back to the apartment at the rear of the restaurant to change into her hostess dress, add makeup to her scrubbed complexion, and twist her hair into a soft chignon.

Mariner's Wharf was even more crowded tonight. Early diners demanded quick service in order to attend the symphony performance at the Civic Center. The late evening customers took their time, relaxing over good food and drink. Mike Harris agreed with Brandy's decision to call in an extra bartender to help with the standing-room-only crowd in the Porthole Lounge.

As of yet, there had been no sign of Griffen. But Brandy found herself too busy to dwell on his absence. The kitchen had exhausted its supply of trout amandine and all the menus needed to be changed. So far the only surprise of the evening had been the arrival of her former employer, Dennis Graham, and his wife, Cynthia.

It was Dennis's husky frame that cornered Brandy in the bar while she waited for a drink order to be filled. "Have you decided to switch careers?" he joked lightly.

"My brother needed assistance," she returned in a cool, even tone. "I hope you and your wife enjoyed your dinner."

"It was excellent as usual." Dennis stared at her perfectly composed features for a moment. "Cynthia and I have been discussing you. She was quite upset to learn you'd quit. We've decided to take you back."

Brandy arched a burnished brow, her blue-gray eyes implacable and unwavering, her voice as sharp as a sword. "Why, Dennis, how very magnanimous of you! Have you just realized your wife doesn't know the difference between chintz and corduroy?" She took a deep, steadying breath. "I've had a lot of time to dissect the situation, and I don't want to come back. You used me and you won't change."

"Things will be different, I promise, Brandy." His deep voice lowered persuasively. "I can guarantee you that raise and. . . ."

With abstract politeness Brandy appeared to listen to the rest of the benefits Dennis was offering, but her gaze soon became preoccupied by a steadily moving masculine figure that was reflected in the large mirror over the bar.

Despite the crush of bodies she instinctively recognized the animal energy contained inside the camel suit. It was Griffen! Adrenaline replaced irritation. The nearer he came, the faster Brandy's pulse beat. Just the sight of him nudged her body chemistry into action. Her skin felt hot and her breathing became shallow. Griffen was now close enough for her lungs to inhale the familiar aroma of his expensive, thin cigar.

Dennis kept repeating her name, anxiously trying to regain her attention. His voice was urgent and the beefy, moist palms that settled on her bare arms only reinforced his uneasiness.

Brandy looked into his hazel eyes and smiled a smile that held mysterious mischief. "Dennis." Her voice turned into a low seductive purr. "I really appreciate your concern and your offer is very tempting."

She smoothly disengaged his hands and let her fingers walk up the arm of his navy blazer to caress his flaccid cheek. Startled, Dennis blinked at her. His heavy jaw slackened under her odd display of affection.

But Brandy knew their tableau was being watched by a pair of eaglelike brown eyes. In a sweet voice laced with a soupçon of vengeance, she delivered her parting blow. "Dennis, I really think you should go back to your wife. Everything is over between us. I've found someone else. Try to forget me." She turned and picked up a brass tray that now held five tall, fruit-garnished piña coladas and quickly made her exit before the confused Dennis had a chance to utter more than her name.

Somehow Brandy managed to serve the drinks and return to the hostess lectern without a single backward glance. Her heart was beating—rapid and urgent beneath the apricot crepe. Casually she turned her head and found Griffen had managed to commandeer a bar stool that allowed him to scrutinize her every move.

Her expression was cool and controlled, a sharp contrast to the tempestuous hurricane raging inside her. Even from a distance, Griffen's raw masculine charm caused her sensual clock to start ticking. Her smoky gaze became hypnotized by his brown eyes. She watched his expression grow derisively mocking.

Eyes agleam, Brandy smiled and accepted the silent challenge. She felt frankly feminine, wantonly daring, and voraciously uninhibited. It was easy for her to make the metamorphosis to coquettish butterfly, flitting from one male customer to another, pollenating their egos with phony titillation.

Twenty minutes elapsed before Brandy had the opportunity to reenter the bar. She deftly insinuated her curvaceous figure next to Griffen's seated form. Her apricot-crepe-encased hip brushed suggestively against his left hand.

Brandy gave the assistant bartender a drink order, then found her diamond-bright eyes snagged by Griffen's reflection in the mirror. He was staring at her. She felt wicked and irresistible. Her tongue languorously moistened her copper-tinted lips. "It's very nice to see you again," she told him in a low, throaty voice.

"I'm surprised I was even noticed," he returned evenly, each word punctuated by aromatic wisps of cigar smoke. "You're very adept at playing to a room of men." He hesitated, his lips twisted mockingly. "Brandy."

"Why, thank you—" she paused dramatically "—Griffen." Brandy watched his dark brow arch in surprise and she smiled. They were now on a first-name basis. It made everything so proper.

"I do enjoy men," she continued in a husky, amused tone, "as long as they have their permanent teeth." Brandy turned; her mouth was partially open. She looked hungry.

Griffen's energies seemed focused on the fullness of her parted lips. He stubbed out his cigar; his breathing was ragged. "I thought you had decided to concentrate your efforts on the owner of the Wharf?"

Brandy leaned toward him, watching his eyes lower to the inviting hollow between her breasts. "I'm still open to other suggestions." Her liberated glands were enjoying the role of seductress.

"And yet you gave your friend Dennis a final good-bye?" His voice roughened impatiently.

Brandy's slim shoulders gave a careless shrug. "I found Dennis and permanence getting to be a bore." She reached for a wooden dish of peanuts to add to the tray bearing a gin and tonic the bartender had brought. "Variety is the spice of life and I lead a very spicy life." Five virile fingers gripped her narrow wrist. Brandy looked at Griffen questioningly.

"Do you mind if I take some?"

"Take anything you'd like."

She was acutely conscious of the rough, calloused hand that lingered for a tantalizing moment against her smooth skin. She watched his long fingers transfer the tiny salted nuts to his tongue.

Brandy decided her eyes must be her second most erogenous zone. They visually devoured and savored every inch of Griffen from the tiny mole at the edge of his left sideburn to the nine gray hairs that blended with the black ones in his thick mustache.

She couldn't resist the temptation to touch him.

She wanted to stroke away the lines of fatigue at the edges of his delicate eyelids, but instead she let her icy peach fingernails smooth the collar of his blue shirt and glide over the knot of his color coordinated striped silk tie.

Now was the perfect time to burst into a fit of girlish giggles, offer to buy him a drink, and tell him how wrong he was. Maybe she could be introduced to the real Griffen and he to the real Brandy.

Griffen turned, his lean face looked carved from granite and his brown eyes cold and uncompromising.

Brandy sighed. "Regretfully I must get back to my duties." She picked up the tray and turned toward the dining room. For the first time since they had met she had spoken the truth. She did regret leaving Griffen.

When Brandy looked back through the arched doorway, she found his bar stool vacant. An empty, aching feeling invaded her body and settled in the pit of her stomach. A dull weariness replaced the glow of excitement.

The kitchen was closed, the staff and waiters had departed, the dining room lay dark and empty. Only the amber-lanterned lounge was left to play reluctant host to a handful of hangers-on. Mike Harris was busy replenishing the liquor stock and Brandy, finished with Sunday's menu changes, had only the bank deposit to get from the office safe before she could tumble into bed.

Smothering a prodigious yawn, she dispassionately eyed the late customers. Brandy stretched her body off the red leather bar stool. "Why don't you see if you can nudge the last of our clientele out the door," she murmured to Mike. His curly red head nodded in quick agreement.

The corrected menus left at the hostess lectern, Brandy's pinched feet carried her weary body across the silent dining room to the business office situated at the far end of the service hallway.

"Calling it a night?"

It was Griffen. Brandy felt her energy return. Slowly her hand slid free of the door latch. She turned, a soft smile curving her full lips as her crystal gaze encountered his rugged physique. "Have you come back to give me another of your late night lectures?"

"No more lectures." He moved closer, his eyes unreadable brown agates in the shadow-strewn hall. "I don't think anyone could dissuade you from your prospective target."

"I'll have to meditate on that." Brandy pouted at him. A mixture of rich tobacco and the royal scent of sandalwood cologne assaulted her senses. The nipples of her breasts swelled against the thin crepe. Desire was growing heartbeat by heartbeat. "Can I offer you a . . . drink?" she inquired, her seductive voice geared to entice him.

"I just came back to say good-bye." The gray light cast the planes and angles of his face a harsh tone, but there was an underlying gentleness in his voice.

"You mean good night," Brandy corrected automatically, trying to ignore the wild, delicious sensations that darted beneath her skin.

Griffen shook his head. "I'm leaving Tampa." He took a deep breath; her perfume enveloped him in a cascade of haunting jasmine notes. He opened his mouth then closed it. He could only stare into the diamond eyes that glittered inches from his own.

A sense of loss invaded Brandy. Griffen was leaving; he would be gone in a matter of minutes. She would never taste his mouth or feel his touch again. She found she desperately needed the fantasy to continue a little longer.

Brandy moved against him, each nerve-ending screaming for bodily contact. "It's a shame you have to leave," she whispered, her fingertips caressing the square line of his jaw to his ear. Her thumb teased the well-formed lobe and the hollows inside.

Griffen meant to disengage himself from her touch. Instead he found his own hands enjoying the silken expanse of golden skin from her neck to her spine. "I doubt you'll even remember me after tonight." The harshness of his voice betrayed the savage turmoil of his emotions.

Her back arched and her pelvis tipped forward. Brandy found receptive pleasure in the friction of two clothed, entwined bodies. The hard length of his body and his touch answered her deepest needs.

Her fingers lifted a vibrant wedge of dark hair at the nape of his neck. "I'll remember you," came her husky promise. What she was saying and doing made no sense. She felt possessed. It was as if another entity had invaded her system. She wasn't going to fight it; she was going to enjoy it.

The soft curves of her body molded against him like a second skin. Her half-hooded eyes ignored the ominously working muscle in his cheek to concentrate on his sensuously curved mouth. When she spoke, her breath mingled invitingly with his. "It's a shame you have to leave. But I don't think you should be penalized for early withdrawal."

Brandy's even white teeth nibbled apart Griffen's lower lip; her teasing tongue slipped into the exciting interior of his mouth. She found he was no longer fighting but embellishing her pleasurable challenge.

Time and circumstances were temporarily obliterated under the tongues that worked feverishly together. Brandy's hand slid beneath his suit jacket, her fingernails scratching an erotic circular pattern along the muscles of his chest.

Griffen's hard frame pressed her obedient body against the carved oak door. His palm stroked the delicate apricot crepe free of her shoulders to let his rough fingers explore the swelling velvet mounds of her breasts. His thumb and forefinger found, then teased, her excited nipples. Her responding moan echoed their mutual pleasure.

Angrily Griffen pulled his lips free, his half-hooded eyes staring into Brandy's smoky orbs. "I must be crazy." He breathed fiercely and moved to jerk his hard body free of its submissive cushion.

Brandy shook her head; her fingers silenced his words and calmed his thoughts, then her hands locked tightly around his neck anxiously pulling his wonderful warm mouth back onto hers.

Thoughts drifted and darted somewhere in the recesses of her mind. She refused to think. She refused to make sense of her unusual actions. She knew only that this man ignited a torrent of hidden sensations that sent a blistering rush of heat to envelop her body.

Griffen stopped ignoring the fever rising within. His lips were hard and demanding while his hands sought to conquer every inch of silken skin.

An obscene, cheery whistle penetrated their intimate surroundings. It was followed by a low baritone voice that called Brandy's name.

"I was wrong," Griffen said roughly, "you're not through for the night." He freed himself from her embrace, his dark eyes surveyed her tall, curvaceous figure one last time. "Good-bye, Brandy."

Outside, the sultry evening breeze did little to quell Griffen's salacious desires; neither did the orange silk rose that was captured in his steellike grip.

Brandy's trembling fingers pushed the loosened strands of hair back into the curve of her chignon. Her passionate dark eyes stared into the empty hallway, trying to recapture time. Only when Mike Harris's shadow loomed against the adjacent wall did Brandy open the office door and step back into reality.

## CHAPTER FOUR

The brown metallic GM van was wedged between a tractor trailer and a Greyhound bus on the traffic-choked Tampa expressway. Brandy didn't mind. The van was air-conditioned, the windows bronzed against the glaring sun, and the radio was playing a soothing stream of classical orchestrations. It felt good to be back in the driver's seat, not only of her auto, but of her life.

Last night, despite being on the brink of physical and mental exhaustion, Brandy had been unable to sleep. The soothing green and beige color scheme of the Wharf's one-bedroom apartment did little to relax her heightened emotions. She sat in the kitchen, draining cups of warm milk, and willing the gently whirling blades of the ceiling fan to hypnotize her into lethargy. But once in bed, the tranquilizing intimacy of the king-size mattress provoked her senses to even greater havoc.

Brandy had only to close her eyes and Griffen's image erupted into three-dimensional clarity, an image so virile that her ears echoed the sound of his deep voice, her nose twitched at the aroma of his tobacco, and her body vibrated against his remembered muscular strength. It was an image potent enough to make her breasts swell against an invisible hand and turn the very core of her femininity into a throbbing mass of unfulfilled desire.

Brandy left the bedroom and sat down on the window seat curling her long legs beneath her, waiting for the pink and pearl dawn to wash away the darkness of a lonely night. Eventually grim reality replaced wanton fantasy as the glittering waters of Tampa Bay once again played host to another day's activities.

For once, Brandy wished she had listened to her mother. Hadn't Mom always warned her never to speak to strangers? But Brandy had done more than just *speak* to Griffen! She had provoked him, enticed him, and blatantly tried to seduce him. And to what end? Griffen was gone and the mystery surrounding him would never be solved.

But Brandy had her own mystery to solve. She had to determine how and why she had lost control of her common sense. She was ashamed of her actions and disgusted by her feelings. Her body had ruled her mind. She had been ready, willing, and positively anxious to satiate her desires in a physical act. She had never thought of having reckless sex with anyone, especially not a man who only exhibited contempt for her.

Not full contempt, she rationalized. Griffen hadn't

fought too hard to control his own urges. He seemed attracted to her "badness," but there were hundreds of things Brandy could have said and could have done to change that image and Griffen's thinking about her.

But most of her personal dealings with men had been full of shoulds and coulds. She didn't need or want a man in her life right now. Her total energy, her total focus was on achieving her career goal. Intimacy fell last on her list of priorities. A relationship that led to permanence would become a part of her world when she had secured her position.

Brandy could only conclude that her glands had been inactive too long and had been awakened by a challenge. Perhaps she shared an affinity with the female alligators that populated Florida. They, too, came alive during the month of April to inspect the males. But any male that could be forced into action too easily was ignored. It was the fighters that were the main attraction, the main challenge. Griffen had certainly put up a good fight and Brandy had never been one to ignore a challenge!

Brandy bypassed the Buccaneer Stadium exit and nosed the van onto the Westshore ramp. It was time to put the excitement of Griffen out of her mind. She had another challenge to meet—that of the elusive St. Clair.

Her interior design portfolio was professional, comprehensive, and impressive. But even more impressive, she prayed silently, were her plans for phase two of St. Clair's Triton Shoals project.

She had christened her work "miniature palaces by the sea." They were just that. Thirty single-family units that made the best of climate, setting, building materials, and natural-energy patterns, concepts that worked with the environment not against it or in spite of it. Each house was an entity unto itself, designed to give its owner a feeling of richness combined with practicality.

The architectural styles were more a smorgasbord of designs that populated the world. There was a Normandy-styled French stucco house, a Cape Cod cottage, a modern rough-hewn cedar and brick, a Spanish hacienda with a red-tiled roof, and twenty-six other modern and classic structures. The most important part was the fact they were all energy-efficient—not the energy hogs that most builders were still making and selling.

In some Brandy used passive solar techniques—orienting buildings east to west, having vestibules that served as air locks, heavy roof and wall insulations, and natural ventilation to keep the houses comfortably cool with minimal or no mechanical air-conditioning.

In others she incorporated a century-old technique —the vented-skin system—that was used in constructing ice houses in the North and would keep houses cool in Florida. The skin system allowed heat to pass between outside and inside walls and exit through ceiling vents.

In all design concepts she used landscaping to provide moisture, shade, and to reduce the surrounding air temperature—double-glazed windows, polyurethane doors, and solar water heating systems made the homes the quintessence of quality. Her interior-design appointments added tasteful sophistication.

76

What if St. Clair had an edifice complex? What if he wanted some awe-inspiring concrete-and-steel creation that would bear his name and stand like a pedestal, rising out of the sand, to weather the eons?

Then he would have to look elsewhere! Brandy grimaced ruefully. She turned the van into the palm-tree-lined parking lot of the towering wedge-shaped Marriott Hotel. At this late date and with her own career plans in limbo, Brandy decided she would jump at the design job. Maybe Daytona Beach would provide her with the intern architect position she so badly needed.

"I'm sorry, Mr. St. Clair is not in." The neatly uniformed information clerk smiled her regret. "Are you Miss Abbott?"

Brandy nodded glumly. She was two hours earlier than expected and St. Clair had told her he was busy with appointments.

"Mr. St. Clair was expecting you for dinner. In fact I've made reservations at the Kastan here in the hotel," continued the pleasant-voiced receptionist, with "Germaine" imprinted on a name tag.

"Unfortunately I have a problem with a dinner meeting," Brandy said with little enthusiasm. "I was hoping . . ." Her voice trailed off and she shook her head. "Never mind. Would you see that Mr. St. Clair gets these two portfolios and this note?"

"Of course." Germaine quickly relieved Brandy of two large design carriers, then deposited the note in the appropriate call box.

Brandy took a conciliatory deep breath. There was nothing she could do about a personal audience with

77

St. Clair. Her work would have to speak for itself. Slowly she retraced her steps across the massive chandelier-dotted lobby. She might as well head back to the Wharf and try to get in a nap before the four o'clock rush of diners arrived.

"I say, Brandy, is that you?"

A very British voice spun her around and the sight of a familiar face, weathered by sun and sea spray, turned her frown into a broad smile. "Admiral Carlsen, what are you doing here?"

"Come, come. I thought we had dispensed with all that stuffy formality." A pair of sea-blue eyes danced into her own surprised eyes. "You were calling me Hank . . . very Yankee."

Brandy laughed. "According to the papers, I should be calling you Sir Henry," she bantered easily. "I see Her Royal Highness finally anointed you Knight of the Bath."

His own mouth creased into a grin. "That's only because I'm still one of the very few rich enough to pay the Crown all those bloody taxes!" Sir Henry appreciatively eyed Brandy's tall figure in the slim beige two-piece sweater dress. "Since when are we so polite? After all, you did live with me for three months." Two arms reached out and crushed her in a strong embrace that turned heads and raised eyebrows in the public lobby.

"Hank!" His name was garbled since Brandy's mouth and nose were pressed tightly against the collar of his double-breasted navy yachting jacket. She twisted free and stared in mock annoyance at his grinning sun-bronzed features. "You British certainly have a very strange sense of humor. How's your wife?"

"Athena has probably bought out most of Acapulco," Sir Henry returned dryly. He consulted an antique gold pocket watch, snapped it shut, then smiled at her. "I've got half an hour before my plane takes off. How about tea?"

Minutes later they were seated in a quiet alcove of the hotel's Sigi Lounge. A waiter hurried to fill their order.

"What are you doing so far from your wife?" Brandy inquired, relaxing into the oversized wicker chair.

"You know how temperamental women can get." Sir Henry sighed, putting the flame of a silver lighter to the fragrant tobacco in his ever-ready pipe.

"Athena? Temperamental?"

"No, no, my dear." He raised his gray brows sharply. "The *Hyperion*. Her two diesel engines have been giving us nothing but trouble. We anchored off Mexico and the maintenance engineer sent me for some blasted part available here only."

A bubble of laughter escaped Brandy's throat. The *Hyperion* was the retired admiral's only child, and he was totally at her mercy. She was a replica of a three-masted clipper ship, reminiscent of the fabled *Flying Cloud*. The 170-foot vessel, needing a crew of fifty-five, had been bought in Miami and Brandy had spent three months designing and refurbishing the various staterooms and saloons aboard.

She had met Sir Henry and Athena, his wife of thirty years, at a yacht party held in Tony's restaurant. The Carlsens had fallen in love with her remodeling work on the Wharf and hired her to work on the *Hyperion*. Brandy had been virtually adopted by the couple and most of the rather aged British crew that attended the magnificent vessel.

"Now tell me." Sir Henry puffed away, taking time to add the perfect mix of milk and sugar to his tea. "What have you been up to? It's been nearly two years since we dropped anchor here."

Brandy frowned, watching a slice of lemon swim around her own steaming beverage. "After two years I was hoping to rattle off quite a list." She sighed and looked at him. "The truth is I've done a lot of design projects, but that architect's license still eludes me."

"Why not take time for a vacation and come with me?" he offered generously. "Athena and I are bound for the South Pacific. Think of the fun you'd have teaching the natives how to build condominium grass huts."

"Don't tempt me, Sir Henry," Brandy returned in a serious voice. "I've just left a new project at the front desk for an East Coast developer. If that falls through, I'm left with nothing. I don't know what I'm going to do."

The admiral's forefinger lifted her bowed head; his thumb settled roughly into the deep dimple in her chin. "Since when have you become a simpering chit?" he growled angrily. "You've got more talent and done more with your talent than most young people your age.

"So you're in a slump." Sir Henry knocked the bowl of his pipe against an ashtray. The tobacco dregs spilled out in a pile. "But, by God, you're not in the slump we were during the Big War. Things

80

looked blacker than black, but then the navy was notified that Winston was back."

Brandy blinked; her eyes grew wide as his voice increased to stentorian proportions. "Churchill wouldn't let us give in to fear. That Winston, what a bulldog! Through blood, toil, tears, and sweat we made it our finest hour." Sir Henry sighed and took a deep breath.

"You Yanks would due well to read British history," he told her with a wide smile. "There's always a way out of any situation. You just have to persevere. You may be without a job, without direction, but, Brandy, never surrender to fear."

She stared at him for a long time, then straightened her backbone against the chair. "You know, you're right, Hank. I've put too much of my heart and my life into architecture to give it up." Brandy's voice grew stronger. "I've been letting other things distract me. But no more! I'm going to persist despite opposition or maybe even because of it."

"That-a girl." The admiral's rich voice cheered her on. "Go after that license with the heart and the roar of a lion."

"I will." Those two words instantly inflamed Brandy's personal commitment to her career.

Sir Henry drained his cup, inspected his treasured timepiece, and sighed. "I must be off. I've got one of your beastly rental cars yet to return."

Arm in arm they walked out of the plant-strewn lounge into the parking lot. Brandy's eyes blinked not only against the sun but against burning tears. "It seems too long between visits. I miss sitting around with that potent rum grog you make, talking and dreaming."

"But your dreams are on their way to becoming reality," Sir Henry reminded her staunchly, then he grinned. "Let me have one more hug to pass on to Athena." He pulled Brandy against the lean length of his body; his fingers combed her thick hair into charming disarray.

"This is our marine cable code, wire if you need us." He handed her a card from his breast pocket then, wiping his own eyes, he hurried toward the opposite end of the parking lot.

Brandy, poised on the edge of the sidewalk searching for her car keys was totally unaware that her actions with Sir Henry had been under clinical observation. It wasn't until a shadow slanted over her shoulder and stayed to block the view of the inside of her purse. She turned and found her eyes tangled with a familiar narrowed gaze.

"I thought you working girls had adopted that never-on-Sunday rule." Griffen's rough voice sneered; his mustachioed mouth twisted derisively.

With incredible poise Brandy was able to mask her shock at seeing him. "Everyone enjoys a little afternoon delight." Her honeyed tone was childlike and quite breathless.

He stared into her sweetly rounded face for a long moment, then shook his head sharply. "My God, he was old enough to be your father!"

Her diamond-bright gaze lowered from his rugged features to the wide shoulders and powerful physique contained in a navy business suit. His body seemed to be talking a silent language to hers; she could feel her inner heat rising and knew it had nothing to do with the sun. An inner devil prompted her words. "Had I known I'd see you again . . ." Brandy let her voice trail off suggestively.

Griffen's hands held a death grip on the handle of his leather attaché case. He willed himself to turn and walk away, but the message his brain sent never reached his feet. "Well, I'm here now and since your libido is already primed, why don't we go inside." His eyes were totally unreadable. "I must admit I'm losing the fight against your obvious charms."

A clammy chill replaced the fever in her veins; her blood pressure dropped, her breathing became labored, and perspiration licked her spine. "I'm afraid my time is all booked up," Brandy returned evenly. She swung her hair back in a careless gesture. "I have an employer to make happy and some very hungry dinner customers." Then that inner devil reared its voice again. "Will I see you later tonight?"

Angry at himself, Griffen took a step back, anxious to be free of her intoxicating karma. "Tonight I'm going to be occupied with a woman who is not only brilliant, but witty and charming and totally dedicated to a legitimate career."

Brandy's eyes opened facetiously wide. "She sounds very prim and proper. You'll be bored. I guarantee it." She watched him turn on his heel and disappear through the automatic door.

For a minute Brandy regretted not accepting his invitation. It would have been heaven to spend time wrapped in his arms, exploring the erotic nooks and crannies of his body, and finding mutual satisfaction.

She mentally slapped herself and purposefully

strode toward her van. Hadn't she just made a promise to persevere toward her goal, to stubbornly avoid any outside influences? She would never surrender to her desires!

Brandy yanked open the door and climbed into the plaid bucket seat. Gunning the engine to life, she decided to stop at a bookshop. Perhaps a volume on Churchill would help her attain her goals and keep the devil in its place.

It proved to be, what Sir Henry would have called, a "beastly night." A continual drizzle of warm rain mixed with the cool surface of the Bay produced a heavy fog that tumbled over the surrounding area. Most of the reservations were canceled and by eleven o'clock, The Wharf was in hibernation until Tuesday's lunch crowd would rouse it from a deserved rest.

Brandy, her engagement as *femme fatale* and hostess over, had planned to drive back to her duplex in Lakeland, but hazardous road conditions made that impossible. Her energy level was unusually high and she prowled around the Wharf's tiny apartment like a caged animal, her only physical activity was chomping on roasted peanuts.

She was extremely pleased that she had been able to exorcise the mysterious Griffen from her mind. Of course, Brandy rationalized, it was probably due to the fact that this was the first evening they had not seen each other.

It was now time to channel all her energies on St. Clair. The developer would have had hours to study her design portfolio and inspect her sketches. Brandy was anxious to know his reaction.

Her blue-gray eyes looked from the cypress wall clock to the beige telephone. Was it too late to call him? Would it be too presumptuous to call him?

Brandy picked up the phone receiver, stared at the tiny gray squares, then punched in her own number. Her answering machine dutifully recited a collection of messages—the last from St. Clair!

"Mr. St. Clair, I just got your message." Brandy's voice erupted in a high staccato across the lines. "I hope I'm not disturbing you." She wriggled uncomfortably despite the fact she was lying in the center of a pillow-strewn bed.

"On the contrary, Miss Abbott, I was hoping to hear from you no matter what the hour," returned his deep baritone voice. "I deeply regret having missed you this afternoon."

Brandy swallowed the nervous lump in her throat. "I . . . I want to apologize for the mix-up," she returned quickly, her fingers twisting the cord into tight little loops. "I had a personal emergency. I hope you understand."

"I understand perfectly." St. Clair's calm tone reached out and bathed her agitation. "I have spent a delightful evening getting to know you through your work. You have great style, Miss Abbott, and I've always felt style is a reflection of a person's intellect and knowledge."

"Why . . . why, thank you," Brandy stammered, her cheeks reddening like a schoolgirl's under his compliments. "My work is very important to me. I

85

put a lot of time, effort, and myself into each assignment."

"Your design portfolio is one of the most varied and extensive I have ever seen. Your letters of reference are impeccable. But I think I'm most impressed by your versatility. You not only decorate homes and business offices, but restaurants, hospitals, bank lobbies, and even a very grand sailing ship."

"I have been very fortunate with projects, Mr. St. Clair," Brandy said with a reminiscent smile. "I thrive on variety, and I enjoy working with people. I take the time to get to know their personalities and study the places I'm to design and decorate."

"I know this is an unfair question, Miss Abbott, but how would you approach decorating the Shoals condos?"

Brandy closed her eyes and tried to visualize the structure. Her mind carefully assembled each thought and each word. "The Shoals and its occupants will live in harmony with the ocean. The sea is a moving landscape. It can soothe and relax or bring force and turmoil. Most people need balance and calm to their harried lives. I would approach the decorating by watching the light at various times of the day and then balance the rooms to achieve a form of serenity no matter what style is used."

St. Clair sounded thoughtful. "I was struck by the photos in your portfolio of the house you designed in the Keys. It reminded me very much of the homes in Greece."

"That's exactly where the plan came from," she told him. "The owners had lived in Rhodes and loved it, so I just transplanted a little of that Aegean look to Florida." Brandy took a deep breath and redirected the conversation away from interiors to exteriors. "I was wondering if you had time to inspect my sketches on Phase Two of the Shoals project?"

The silence on the phone was deafening. Brandy could feel her pulse jump in her throat and her body felt chilled. When St. Clair did speak, he seemed to be choosing his words with utmost care. "It is a very interesting and unique idea, Miss Abbott."

She gave a silent groan and waited for that horrendous word, "but," to assault her ears and crush her self-esteem.

"You have incorporated every energy-efficient product currently available," he continued in a solemn voice, "and encompassed old techniques that have been ignored in the wake of modern accomplishments." St. Clair paused; his voice seemed to grow introspective. "By developing the land into single-family units, I would be relieved of future responsibilities."

Brandy's smooth forehead puckered in contemplation. "You make that sound very important."

"It is, at least to me." He gave a self-conscious laugh. "I don't believe I mentioned that I am a lawyer. In handling this land-developing, my client list has tumbled into near oblivion. I enjoy trial work much more than being the proverbial real estate tycoon, despite the fact that I worked my way through college on construction jobs."

"We have much in common, Mr. St. Clair," Brandy said evenly. "Design and decorating jobs paid for my architectural studies. But I am determined to gain my license by the end of this year."

"I find your attitude commendable and as impressive as your work. I think you'll be pleased to learn that I have sent copies of your plans to the architectural firm in Daytona that is handling the Shoals project."

Brandy sat up with a jerk, her eyes wide in surprise. "I . . . I am very flattered, Mr. St. Clair."

"I am not trying to flatter you, Miss Abbott. You demonstrate a great deal of aesthetic tolerance in your work and your research is astounding."

"Thank you," she returned simply. It was difficult to contain her excitement and remain professional in the wake of his announcement. "I can promise, if I am hired, you can be assured that you will get my total concentration and my total energy."

"Your enthusiasm is infectious." St. Clair's voice lost its sober business tone and turned warm and inviting. "I happen to be free tomorrow morning, I'd like very much to have brunch with you."

"Thank you, I'd like that too," Brandy responded with undisguised appreciation.

"Fine. I'll make reservations for eleven at the restaurant here in the hotel. See you tomorrow. Good night, Miss Abbott."

Brandy tumbled back amid the bed pillows. "Mr. St. Clair, you are a man after my own heart!" Her mouth split into a Cheshire-cat grin. It was wonderful to find a man so supportive, so encouraging, and so complimentary!

Tomorrow his attractive, deep voice and his sensitive, positive personality would be transformed into a masculine, physical presence. Anticipation erupted inside of Brandy. She was anxious for tomorrow—anxious to be introduced to the flesh and blood St. Clair. A peculiar warmth assailed her muscles and intoxicated her senses.

No! She scolded herself sharply. This was purely a business relationship. There would be no personal involvement. It was a rule she had made and always adhered to from the very beginning of her design career. It was too easy to become involved in people's lives, especially when you were around them constantly and working on their environment.

Brandy sat up, Indian style, and reached for a handful of peanuts. St. Clair would be a man to cultivate as a friend and confidant. She popped the nuts carelessly into her mouth. They shared the same attitudes, he was easy to talk to, and very understanding.

Her back molars pulverized the nutmeat; then suddenly a sharp pain knifed through her upper jaw into her left eye. Brandy scrambled off the bed and ran to the bathroom and carefully brushed her teeth. It was impossible to check her molar, but when she breathed in air, the pain was even sharper.

By eight the next morning Brandy had consumed two dozen aspirins, half of which were dissolved on her aching tooth. Her cheek was swollen and she looked remarkably like she did when she was ten and had mumps!

She stared at the telephone. She had two calls to make—her dentist and St. Clair. The last was infinitely more painful.

"Miss Abbott, you sound terrible!"

"I feel terrible, Mr. St. Clair," Brandy mumbled through her discomfort. "I'm afraid I won't be able to make brunch; I have a dental problem." She held her breath for his response.

"I'm sorry, I hope you feel better." St. Clair was silent for a moment. "I was just rechecking my schedule and I'm filled with appointments until Wednesday, which is my last day in Tampa. Could we meet, say one o'clock at . . . why not at Tony's restaurant, is that convenient?"

"That would be wonderful. Thank you so much for understanding." Brandy sank onto the edge of the bed, her disposition rapidly improving.

"Not at all, actually the more we keep prolonging our meeting, the more intrigued I become. I'm afraid I'm expecting quite a lot from you." His voice had an amused lilt to it. "You're quite the mystery lady."

"Right now I'm a swollen-jawed lady. But again, thank you for your patience."

"I'll see you in two days, Miss Abbott."

## CHAPTER FIVE

"Well, Mr. Cameron, marital bliss certainly becomes you!" Brandy teased her elder brother, her own face a reflection of his smiling features. She was relieved to see the gaunt, haggard lines that had prematurely aged his face had been replaced by a glow of youthful exuberance.

"Miss Abbott, I feel like a new man," Tony returned with an easy grin before leading Brandy through the Wharf's crowded dining room to his office.

"I am very glad I listened to your lectures, little sister," Tony admitted, pausing in the middle of the service hallway. "Rita and I spent this past weekend really communicating our feelings and our thoughts. We discovered we had too many pluses to dissolve our marriage."

Tony rubbed his jaw. "I never realized just how long it had been since we had really talked about our problems and fought over them as well. We were occupying the same house and sharing the same bed but not relating to each other's personalities." He smiled into Brandy's suspiciously moist blue-gray eyes, his own alight with happiness. "The most startling revelation came early this morning. You are going to be an aunt!"

Brandy's jaw dropped; she blinked in surprise. "That's fantastic, congratulations!" She wrapped her arms around Tony's neck and nearly crushed him in her excitement. "How long has Rita known?"

"Apparently that was one of the reasons why she moved out." He paused and took a deep breath. "Rita found out she was pregnant, casually broached the subject of children one night, and I, like a jerk, gave her my ever-ready speech about overpopulation, wanting to be free, seeing all the infanticide during 'Nam, and so forth." Suddenly Tony turned very serious. "But don't think I decided to patch things up because of the baby. Mom made that mistake and stayed with my father longer than she should have. Rita kept her secret until this morning."

"Have you called Mom?"

Tony laughed. "Yes, she is delighted at being a grandmother. She and Brandon are driving over this weekend. I thought we'd have a family reunion."

"Brandy's long fingers caressed her brother's lean face. "I am so pleased that everything worked out for you. It may be your child that changes the world."

Tony's cheeks took on a faint stain of color. "That's exactly what I said to myself while shaving this morning!" He placed his hands on the shoulders of Brandy's pewter suit jacket and judiciously examined her upturned face. "How's the tooth?"

She gave a wry grimace. "It serves me right for ignoring all those messages Mr. Tooth Decay kept zapping into my jaw. That tooth had been tender for a month. I deserved the abscess, but luckily the antibiotics brought down the swelling and the dentist was able to save the molar." Brandy sighed and looked toward the closed office door. "I hope St. Clair doesn't think I am this incompetent about my work. I was so embarrassed at having to cancel another meeting with him."

"He just arrived a few minutes ago," Tony told her. "By all indications he is very pleased with the quality of your work. It looks as though the interior design job is yours."

"Is that your personal, prejudicial assumption?" she countered dryly.

Tony smiled at her; his long fingers straightened the narrow bronze ribbon tied under the collar of her mustard blouse. "He said as much." Tony gave an abstract shrug. "For some reason, St. Clair was a little abrupt with me, but he raved about your portfolio. You seemed to have made quite an impression on the telephone."

Brandy dimpled prettily. "I can be the essence of charm when I try." She glanced at the digital time display on Tony's watch. "I had better get in there; I don't dare be even a second late."

Tony walked her to the office door and reached to twist open the brass latch.

"I just want to thank you again for taking the restaurant over this weekend. I still feel terribly

93

guilty. This place is a lot of work and I know you didn't need the extra burden."

Brandy turned her head and smiled at him. "I really enjoyed it. I got to wear all my evening finery, play hostess-with-the-mostest, and meet some very interesting people." Her knee pushed the door open. "It was fun while it lasted!" She blew a saucy kiss at his departing, laughing figure, then took a deep breath. Thoughts of fun and frippery faded—Brandy was now the consummate businesswoman. B. J. Abbott was a professional!

She walked into the office and closed the door, but the minute her diamond-bright eyes encountered the man seated behind the desk, Brandy's poise and breath were literally knocked from her body.

Icy anger etched a lean, mustachioed face into even crueler lines. He rose like a monolith from the confines of the red leather chair and slowly walked around the massive oak desk. "You are B. J. Abbott —Brandy?"

She nodded, feeling extremely dull-witted. "You . . . you're St. Clair—Griffen?" Brandy didn't need his curt nod to confirm the punchline to a rude joke.

They stared at each other, unwilling and unable to believe whom they were seeing. His stony brown gaze sized up the incredulous blue-gray eyes of his adversary. They were like two prize fighters weighing each other's mettle—watching, calculating, and waiting for the first punch.

For a split second Brandy's composure faltered under Griffen's harsh, forbidding features. Then her intimidation fled. She masked her consternation with a bold aggressive stance of self-control. Brandy silently blessed the instinct that had directed her to choose a pair of three-inch-high pumps for the interview. Her own considerable height put her on equal level with Griffen's towering masculinity.

"It was fun while it lasted!" Griffen's caustic voice struck the first blow, imitating Brandy's departing comment to Tony. His cold gaze insolently raked every inch of her stiffly erect figure. Her molten-streaked sable hair had been combed into a pristine pageboy, her makeup was soft, and the classic, tailored business suit cleverly concealed the wealth of feminine curves that his hands had intimately explored.

Griffen clenched his fists, angry at his body's instant response to her physical presence and to his own memories. His voice was an animal's snarl. "Now I know why you were so anxious to please a prospective employer. Tony's back with his wife and you need another fish for your hook!"

The challenging light that had invaded Brandy's eyes disintegrated under the superior assurance radiating from Griffen's cynical features. She intently examined the individual shag fibers twisting from the gold carpet. Her peripheral vision watched a pair of tan trouser-clad legs circle her like a buzzard ready to swoop on a near-dead prey.

"You worked so hard over the phone. It must have been exhausting for you to keep up that cultured, business image," Griffen continued in a ruthless voice laced with sarcasm. "You analyzed my every response and cleverly said exactly what I wanted to hear. You're sharp all right."

"You know something, Miss Abbott—" he fairly

spat out her name as though trying to rid his mouth of something foul and unclean "—I was ready to hire you, sight unseen. I was convinced that your work reflected you as a person. Everything I saw was quality."

Griffen walked back to the desk and stared down at Brandy's open portfolio. "I was ready to commit myself, my company, my finances, and my other employees to back your single-family housing development." He shook his head sharply, then took a silver cigar case from the inside of his navy blazer.

A slim lighter ignited the expensive cigar. "I have always believed in fate." Griffen's eyes narrowed against the soft swirls of aromatic smoke to level on Brandy's downbent head. "She's one lady who's blessed me over the years. I had another meeting scheduled for this time and I was going to leave you an apologetic note and a signed contract. Luckily that meeting was canceled."

Griffen looked down at the design sketches, his face twisting in disgust. "I wonder if any of these ideas are even yours!" He slammed the portfolio closed. "And those references. How many of them were procured in the bedroom?" His mouth twisted into a sneer indicative of his contempt. "I don't think I have ever met a more unscrupulous, mercenary, depraved, or dishonest woman. Everything about you is a lie."

Brandy's head snapped up. Angry fires licked her adrenaline into action. Her silence had been an expression of her scorn, but St. Clair was taking it as an admission of guilt. She was guilty about her behavior, but she refused to let him malign her work.

Brandy counted to ten, then swore. The four-letter expletive shocked even her and effectively shut him up.

"Why, you despicable hypocrite!" Her pride and spirit roared with the boldness of a lion. She cut him with his own words. "Sunday night I was innovative, versatile, and talented. But today—today my morals negate my talent!"

She reached out and snatched her case from the desk. "How dare you slander my work," Brandy hissed, her eyes narrowed into twin slits of silver. "I will sue you for libel. Everything is original. Nothing I have ever done or will ever do is a forgery or a plagiarism in any shape or form. As for my references—" She squared her shoulders, tossed her head back, and glared at him. "They are honest and given with appreciation for jobs well done. No one could do your project any better, and you damn well know it!"

Brandy took another deep breath and tried to bring herself under some measure of control. Revenge proved to be her next catalyst.

"Just how tarnish-free is your halo, Mr. St. Clair?" Brandy returned in a low, scathing voice. She attacked again, this time with a more cunning battle plan. "As I recall, you were quite ready to contribute to my delinquincy on several occasions."

She was rewarded by the sight of a mottled red stain creeping up his neck from beneath the collar of his pale blue shirt. "You've got gall to stand there like some . . . some tin god and pass judgment on my morals."

Amid the gray cells of her mind, Brandy realized

it was easier to keep good character than to recover it. She could parade in Tony, her police-commissioner father, her minister, even her physician, but Griffen St. Clair would only damn the truth. In all honesty her greatest character assassin was her own conscience. She may be a sinner, but he was in no position to cast the first stone!

"Men can use women any time and in any way they like." Brandy shrewdly surveyed his impassive features and his rigid demeanor. "And your male chauvinistic body was damn anxious to bed me Sunday afternoon. And you hold yourself up as such a perfect specimen!"

Brandy stared at him for a long moment. She had defeated him by degrees, trumping his every point, but her elevation was turning sour. She hated scenes like this, it humiliated both parties, and neither of them deserved this barrage of vindictive insults.

"Talk about fate!" Brandy turned and headed for the door. Her body was tempered with pride, but she knew her spirit was ready to crumble. She cherished the one remaining privilege of her gender—a good cry in the ladies' room.

"Halt!"

She stopped.

"Come back here."

Brandy stared at the carved wooden door until it blurred, her fingers trembling against the cool brass latch. She took a deep breath and turned.

"Sit down."

She squared her shoulders and stood her ground. She didn't like the military commands he was issuing. "I am not in your platoon, Mr. St. Clair," she reminded him stiffly.

He took a deep breath. "Please." Griffen's vocal cords had great difficulty giving birth to the word. It did move Brandy. He watched her as she sat down.

Uncomfortably perched on the edge of a gold leather reception chair, Brandy warily studied Griffen's enigmatic expression.

It was impossible to discern his next move. She needed an edge and decided on an old but effective ploy.

Brandy placed her portfolio and her gray leather handbag on the corner of the desk. She watched his gaze shift to the neat but large satchel and smiled slightly. A woman's purse was an extension of herself. It gave Brandy a partner and St. Clair another adversary.

Griffen cleared his throat and pressed the tips of his fingers together. He looked from the purse to Brandy then over her head to the sextant mounted on the far wall. "I would like to apologize for the crass remark about your work." He again cleared his throat; his gaze strained to remain distant. "I have no intensions of slandering your work. My own architects have spent the last two days studying your designs and were very impressed."

Brandy gave a regal nod of acceptance at his obviously reluctant apology. Her cautious eyes became fascinated with Griffen's every gesture. She watched his large capable hands reach for the hammered silver cigar case. His long, virile fingers selected a thin cheroot, tamped the ends, then slowly stroked the dark tobacco wrapping before placing it between his firm lips.

Her brain registered his every movement in slow motion. Griffen's calloused but tender fingers had caressed her from the base of her neck down the supple length of her spine. An immediate anatomical response was triggered. Brandy's breathing became shallow; her pulse hammered rapidly against the thin blue-veined skin of her wrist. Her skin took on a rosy glow, the nipples of her breasts tingling against their silk covering, excited by the sensual memory of his further exploration.

Griffen's deep voice punctured Brandy's erotic daydream. "I am trying to understand how you succeeded in your . . . er . . . libertine, Bohemian lifestyle." He inhaled a contemplative lungful of smoke. The exhaled fragrant cloud lingered to tantalize Brandy's olfactory sense before drifting toward the ceiling duct.

"You are obviously well educated. You have a brilliant mind and a unique talent. I don't know why you feel that you have to include your body as an incentive for prospective clients."

Griffen leaned back against the leather cushion, his brown eyes inevitably finding their way to Brandy. He surveyed her round, childlike, flushed features and the downbent head. She looked very vulnerable and in need of protection. "I can only assume that your lack of self-esteem and poor moral judgment stems from an unhappy childhood."

Griffen rubbed his jaw; his thumb and forefinger smoothed his thick black mustache. When he spoke, his voice was warm and conciliatory. "I had a very happy childhood. My parents not only loved me, but they loved each other, and they weren't afraid to show their love. I quite erroneously assume that everyone had such happy formative years."

The tobacco crackled as he took a final drag from his cigar. "I would guess that you came from a broken home. Parents who didn't care about each other or you. You probably got in with the wrong crowd in school, ran wild and undisciplined. The constant parade of men in your life is just a feeble attempt at trying to grab all the love you never had."

Brandy stared at him in abject amazement. Thirty minutes ago he had condemned her very existence and called her every derogatory name he could think of. Now he was finding excuses for her behavior—talk about convoluted logic!

"The army did wonders with recruits whose lives were in worse condition than yours, Brandy."

She blinked in disbelief. "Are . . . are you suggesting that I enlist?" The words were uttered slowly.

"No, no, of course not," Griffen returned quickly. He placed his palms flat on the desktop and pinned Brandy with a sharp glance. "I do think you need some behavior modification. I think you need guidance and constant daytime activity so that you'll be too tired to do anything but sleep when you go to bed at night."

Griffen pushed himself to his feet. "I think you're worth saving. I think putting all that energy you possess to work on my condo project would be just the thing to straighten you out." A peremptory finger was poked under her nose. "I'm going to reform you!"

Brandy resisted the urge to sink her even white teeth into his offending hand. She swallowed the facetious remark she had been about to utter and mentally examined the situation.

She had endured Griffen's supercilious, presumptuous lecture for only one reason—the design project. Now it was hers, if she went along with his demands. It may be callow, shallow, and extremely self-centered, but Brandy's first objective was obtaining her architect's license. Her second would be to teach this arrogant "saint" a lesson!

Dark-fringed lids lowered to conceal her wickedly glittering eyes. Brandy leaned back in her chair, unbuttoned her suit jacket, and crossed her legs high at the knee. She deftly inched her gray skirt higher to reveal an inviting expanse of silk-covered thigh. "I don't know, Griffen—" she gave a long desolate sign "—do you . . . do you really think you could help me?"

With great difficulty Griffen tore his gaze away from her softly pouted mouth and the full, rounded curves of her breasts. He picked up an ivory-handled letter opener and made an intense study of its carved handle. "You are going to be much too busy to think of anything but all the work that has to be done." He privately conceded his words were as double-edged as the opener he held. Perhaps he could purge himself of the attraction Brandy held.

Griffen cleared his throat; his voice was stern. "I expect to have the decorating completed within the six-week time limit. You'll also be working with my architects as they go over your designs step-by-step."

Brandy was literally intoxicated with delight. The

interior design project and her apprenticeship with the architectural firm were going to be the proverbial piece of cake compared to the restructuring needed on herself.

Her life had been tempered by strict parental upbringing, common sense, and a stringent code of ethics. Now her intrepid energies would have to work overtime to turn a feminist into a salacious nymphomaniac. Well, there was no time like the present to launch the first battle in the war between the sexes!

Brandy lifted her arms in a graceful arc over her head. Her full breasts strained and nearly separated the tiny silk buttons on her blouse. "Daytona Beach." Her tongue languorously circled her peach-tinted lips, savoring the word like it was a delicious confection. "Twenty-three miles of hard-packed drivable beach, the fantastic boardwalk, all that wild night-life." Her gaze slanted toward Griffen. "I'm getting excited already!"

Griffen grabbed her wrists and roughly hauled her to her feet. "Oh, no," he growled forcefully, his piercing brown eyes searing the smile of pleasure from her lips. "I'm going to make sure you toe a damn strict line, young lady! You are going to be busy to the point of exhaustion. I own you body and soul. You'll find all agony and no ecstasy on this job!"

Brandy ignored the icy anger etched on his lean face. She stepped closer to his muscular frame, her mouth a whisper's distance from his. "Griffen," she purred, her minty breath disturbing the hairs on his mustache, "all work and no play makes Brandy a very dull girl."

His large hands curved over her shoulders in a punishing grip. "Then dull and bored you'll be!" He gave her a neck-snapping shake. "In six weeks I'll have one of the most outstanding condos on the beach and you'll be a candidate for the convent! Remember, Brandy, I expect you to—"

A loud rap on the door interrupted Griffen. Tony walked into the office carrying a food-laden tray and wearing a blatantly happy expression. "I thought you two would appreciate some lunch," he announced, completely oblivious to the tense atmosphere. "How's everything going?" He set his burden on a side table and smiled at them.

Griffen released his hold on Brandy and moved away. "We've finished," he returned curtly. "Miss Abbott, you have one week to put your . . . *affairs* in order. My office will forward all the information you'll need for the move. I expect you in Daytona on May Day." Without the courtesy of a good-bye, Griffen stalked out of the room.

"May Day, huh?" Brandy pushed up the sleeves of her suit jacket, walked over, and slammed the door shut. "He's the one who is going to be yelling 'mayday' when I get through with him!" Her steel-like gaze smoldered with revenge.

Tony blinked rapidly and scratched his head. "I get the feeling I've entered the Twilight Zone."

"Boy, did you set me up!" Brandy turned the force of her pent-up emotions on her confused brother. "You said St. Clair was fair and understanding, not a prejudicial bone in his body." She pointed to the door, her long forefinger stabbing into space. "That man . . . that man is a patronizing, chauvinistic,

104

condescending, smug, overbearing . . . ugh!" She clamped her mouth shut and paced off her anger.

"Would you like to explain what the hell happened in here?" Tony asked, completely mystified by her attitude. "You arrived so eager and happy and you obviously took the job."

"Of course I took the job," Brandy all but shouted. "Do you think I would let that . . . that man's attitude stop me?" You should have heard that hypocrite," she ground out sharply. "Over the phone I was talented, my work was fantastic, everything about me was perfection itself. But when he found out it was me! Then I was a grasping, mercenary tramp!" She drew herself up to her full, considerable height. "I have been dealing with sexual harassment and innuendos for most of my career. Well, we'll just see how St. Clair takes to being harassed." Her hand curled into a fist. "He's going to be made an example of!"

"Whoa!" Tony reached out and grabbed her clenched hand and led her to a chair. "I can't believe all this happened on your first meeting."

"It was the first meeting of St. Clair and B. J. Abbott but not between Griffen and Brandy!" she fumed, reluctant to settle her agitated body on the leather cushion. "He's been a rat ever since Friday afternoon. Had I known it was him—"

Tony's whistle cut through her jumbled statements. "From the beginning, if you please." He handed his sister a tall, ice-filled glass of mint-garnished tea.

Brandy took a deep, calming breath, exhaled slowly, then gulped down three mouthfuls of the cool liquid. "The beginning was on Friday when your friend, a man I knew only as Griffen, overheard my conversation with Dennis Graham. But Griffen put his own interpretation on what he heard and thought I was ending an affair with a married man, not quitting a job. Then when he came back to the Wharf that night for dinner and found I was the hostess, he accused me of all sorts of things, not the least of choosing you as my next victim!"

Tony stared at his sister's angry features, then laughed. "Well, why in hell didn't you set him straight?"

"Why should I?" Brandy countered defensively. "He's the one who embellished his own lie and turned it into every man's favorite fantasy. Griffen never even asked for my side of the story. He assumed, judged, and condemned."

Brother eyed sister with a shrewdness that came from years of knowledge. "Brandy, just how much did you do to enflame Griffen's fantasy?"

She opened her mouth then closed it, but the telltale blush of color that stained her cheeks spoke a wealth of words. "That's not the point," Brandy retorted stubbornly. "Griffen convicted me on circumstantial evidence. He was the one who pinned on the labels, and all the time he was condemning my so-called lack of morals, that hypocrite was trying to get a piece of my action."

It was Tony's turn to gape in astonishment. He reached over and took a glass of iced tea for himself. "Listen, don't you think this little mix-up has gone on too long? I'm going to call Griffen and explain. You can both get a good laugh out of it and start your new job off on the right foot." He put his glass down and reached for the desk phone.

Brandy's hand blocked him. "Oh, no. You are going to stay completely out of this," she announced in a tone of deadly calm. "Griffen St. Clair thinks of women as though they were . . . those damn cigars he smokes, all laying in a neat row, waiting to be selected, set afire, and discarded when the flame burns out. Well, let's just see how close to the flame old Griffen can get before he gets singed!"

"Brandy," Tony jumped in hastily, "revenge usually backfires. Griffen is no kid; he's been around. I think you're going to find he can take and give a lot of heat."

A smile spread like syrup across Brandy's face. "He's not the saint you think he is, brother. Maybe he believes the worst of me because that's what he desires the most."

"And just how desirous are you willing to be?" came his dry rejoinder.

"Virtue has its degrees and Griffen is soooo anxious to reform me—" her benign expression grew sardonic "—I'm going to let him." Brandy looked down at her hand and twisted the gold zodiac signet ring. "He deserves the sting of this Scorpio!"

Tony cleared his throat and shook his head, but a smile threatened his mouth. "This is the first time I have ever heard you put anything else before your career. Maybe Griffen *will* reform you."

Brandy gave a low chuckle. "Oh, no. That design job will give me a client list, and the internship will get me my license. Griffen is going to get a headache." She looked inquiringly at the tray of food. "Suddenly I'm starved."

Tony wagged his finger at her. "Brandy, you are truly a designing woman!"

## CHAPTER SIX

Daytona Beach—the birthplace of speed. Speed seemed to be all around, Brandy noted wryly. She deftly accelerated her compact van out of the stampeding interstate traffic and executed a rather perilous curve onto the exit ramp that led to Volusia Avenue. There she found herself surrounded by a more lucrative form of speed—money-making sports.

The dogtrack was on her right. It was home to the streamlined, wasp-waisted Greyhounds, the fastest dogs in the world. Parimutuel wagering on the animals was a one-billion-dollar-a-year industry in Florida. Millions came to cheer as their favorite dog pursued a mechanical rabbit around a quarter-mile oval at speeds of forty miles per hour.

Brandy's peripheral vision was caught by a vivid array of colored banners fluttering in the breeze. The massive orange Jai Alai Fronton loomed on her left;

it played host to the only sport in the world where man bets on men. Brandy had become fascinated with the ancient Basque game that closely resembled handball. It was the fastest game in the world and some of her own hard-earned salary had contributed to the billion dollars wagered on the sport in Florida. The clean-cut, mostly Spanish players strapped a basketlike cesta on their arm and propelled a hard ball, the pelota, at their opponents. The pelota has been clocked at over one hundred fifty miles an hour.

A traffic signal halted Brandy's progress in front of the real birthplace of speed—the Daytona International Speedway. Auto racing was a part of Daytona's heritage. Early racers had used the twenty-three-mile-long stretch of hardpacked beach sand to set records and advance the sport. Today the Daytona Speedway played host to the best and the fastest stock cars in the world.

Brandy had missed the twenty-four hours of Daytona in February but had been an avid fan at the Firecracker 400 last July Fourth. She and a record-breaking crowd watched the stock cars—ordinary sedans whose engines and structure had been altered to provide increased power and speed—set record times at over two hundred miles per hour on the dangerous high-banked curves of Daytona.

Speed, energy, excitement—it was contagious! It exhilarated the spirit and sparked the soul. Brandy was finding it difficult to suppress a sudden, overwhelming urge to play hotrod. She hunched over the steering wheel; her eyes sharply watched the traffic light. Fortunately a sheriff's patrol car proved to be the perfect antidote to a short-lived racing career.

The mainland became a far-off blur in the rearview mirror as Brandy sedately headed the van across the palm-tree-lined bridge over the Halifax River to the Peninsula. The Peninsula was the pulse of the city and catered to every whim of the millions of tourists who came to Daytona each year.

Atlantic Avenue was a mixture of fabulous hotels, towering condominiums, restaurants, souvenir shops, and wide-open nightlife. Daytona, like Ft. Lauderdale, had just said good-bye to the Easter invasion of overzealous college students. But the city wasn't getting much opportunity to take a breather, the boardwalk was crowded with people.

Brandy joined a slow line of cars that were intent on entering the access ramp to the beach. She found she was as anxious as the rest for her tires to make contact with the sand on the world's most famous drive-on beach.

A T-shirt-clad, man-sized rat waved at her. Brandy grinned and returned his cheery greeting. She watched the rat, Big Daddy Rat, dance along the sidewalk, swinging his tail, and directing the tourists inside the door of the Rat's Hole, a world-renowned T-shirt emporium. The whisker-preening rat made Brandy think of her new employer—Griffen St. Clair!

Or maybe, she grimaced with rueful honesty at her reflection in the side mirror, it was she who had grown from a mouse into a rat! Tony and her father had thought so, and they both had been quite vocal about it. Her sister-in-law, Rita, had shared her outrage over Griffen's hypocritical stance and had urged her to teach him a lesson. Her mother was more amused by the whole situation, but had warned Brandy to temper her every move with common sense.

Common sense—she wasn't sure what that was anymore. It seemed her reputation wasn't the only thing she had lost last week. Her own life was more complicated and her feelings more chaotic than she could ever remember. While her career was finally motivated in an upward direction, Brandy found she was more excited about her impending relationship with Griffen.

She had ultimately decided during the five-hour drive to Daytona to adjust her behavior to Griffen's attitude. Let him be the catalyst. That would seem the least margin for error. *Do unto others*—how could she go wrong?

But a lot had gone wrong already! Brandy had stopped trying to deny that Griffen St. Clair was able to register a sizable jolt on her personal Richter scale. For years her career and superficial male friendships had given her satisfaction.

It was a shock to her system to realize that this man seemed to be able to summon such intense feelings. The times they had been together her heightened emotions had paralyzed her mental abilities and left no line of demarcation between right and wrong.

They were mentally and emotionally involved already—what would be the consequences of a physical relationship? The idea wasn't repulsive; in fact Brandy found it downright appealing! Would Griffen try to consume her or pleasure her? Perhaps a little of both. For a long time Brandy had relied on the word "no" as her major contraceptive; this time she made sure she was totally protected.

The invigorating scent of tangy salt air filled her lungs as the fascinating grace and force of the Atlantic Ocean became visible through the windshield. On the horizon the sea and the sky rolled into one, edged with a pale blue mist and dazzled by a silent sun.

The parade of tires seemed to violate the serenity of the beach, but the gently lapping tide crawled under the cars and quickly healed the wounds they had made. Brandy watched the white sandpipers dart between the cars to hunt through the ribbed sand, searching the tiny shells for food.

The wide shoreline was peppered with bathers who had been seduced by the warm golden sun and the rolling surf. Colorful Frisbees whirled through the air, surfers tried vainly to tame the waves, and numerous young architects were busy constructing castles in the sand. Nature's tropical beauty was a difficult invitation to reject. It took all of Brandy's considerable willpower not to pull over, park, and join the Sunday afternoon crowd.

The drive down the beach was slow but enchanting. The western skyline was filled with sprawling hotels, towering condominiums, and majestic private homes. A large yellow billboard informed Brandy that this was the last exit off the beach and she reluctantly turned the van back onto the main highway.

A mile down the road she entered the driveway of the Sundial Seaside Motel. One of its white and blue shuttered cottages was to be her home for the next six weeks. The units were surrounded by gracefully swaying palms and cypress trees; colorful hibiscus and fragrant orange blossoms added charm to the rustic beauty of the weathered cabins.

The manager's office was comfortably air-conditioned but empty. Brandy could hear the sounds of a sports program through a closed blue curtain; she hesitated a moment before the palm of her hand connected with the service bell on the desk.

A petite lady, her gray hair in a tight perm, appeared. Brandy lifted her aviator sunglasses to the top of her head and smiled. "Hello, I'm Miss Abbott. I believe you have a reservation for me through St. Clair Construction."

"Sure do, girl, but we weren't expecting you till tomorrow." The woman's angular face broke into a friendly grin. "Herb!" She shouted into the back room, then wiped her hands on the flowered apron that covered her striped housedress. "I'm Gladys Sullivan," she announced, eagerly pumping Brandy's outstretched hand. "If I can get that husband of mine away from the Yankees, you can meet him. Herb!"

"I'm comn'. Where's the fire?" A short, stocky man pushed apart the blue drapes. His dark eyes peered at Brandy over the tops of his reading glasses. A sun-spotted hand quickly reached up to rearrange the few strands of yellow-gray hair that attempted to cover a mostly bald pate.

"Herb, this here's Griffen's friend, Miss Abbott." Gladys smiled at Brandy. "Herb's a might deaf. You have to shout to get his attention."

"You're the one who's wearin' the hearin' aide, Gladys," he snapped back quickly. He looked Brandy up and down, his keen gaze encompassing her lithe figure in its brown T-shirt and beige jeans.

114

"There ain't nothin' wrong with my ears or my eyes." His house-slippered feet shuffled forward; his hand returned Brandy's grip with surprising strength. "Welcome to Daytona, young lady."

"Thank you." Brandy found herself blushing at the elderly couples' undisguised scrutiny. "I'm sorry if my arriving a day early is inconvenient. I could spend the night somewhere else," she offered with a ready smile.

"What for?" Herb blinked owlishly at her. "You're the only guest we've got."

"I . . . I am?" Brandy stammered in surprise. She looked to the husband-and-wife team for an explanation.

"Now, Herb, she's gonna think she's walked into an Alfred Hitchcock movie!" Gladys Sullivan quickly patted Brandy's arm and gave her a reassuring smile. "We sold the place to Griffen's dad early last year. It's gonna be a part of the Shoals—a park I think. Right now only eight cottages are left out of the original twenty. We keep 'em just for people like you who come to work on the construction site. Most have families and only stay with us until they can find a house to rent."

"And what about you two? What are your plans once the motel comes down?"

"We bought one of them condos," Herb told Brandy. His arm snuck around his wife's ample waist and gave her a squeeze. "We're gonna let someone else do all the work for a change."

"That sounds like the perfect way to retire." Brandy smiled at the obviously content couple. "I guess I get my pick of the cabins?"

"Well, we thought you might like a little privacy," Gladys replied in a more serious tone. "Griffen told us all the work you'd be doin'." She eyed Brandy closely and shook her head. "Girl, you're gonna need peace and quiet at night. We put you in the back cottage away from the highway. It's on the highest dune, so that you won't hear the people on the beach too much either."

"It's also the biggest cabin," Herb hastened to add. "We put in an extra dresser, a work table, and more lights. You just ask for whatever else you need. You're part of the family when you stay with the Sullivans." Just yell for Gladys or Herb, and we'll come a-runnin'."

"That's very kind and very appreciated. Please call me Brandy." She easily responded to their hospitality.

Gladys beamed at her. "Your cabin's all set. I'll be changin' the linen and the towels and cleanin' every day—" she held up a peremptory hand "—but, don't you worry, I won't touch nothin'. I just rearrange the dust."

Brandy laughed. "That's fine. If it's in the wastebasket, go ahead and throw it out, but I do have a tendency to spread my work around."

"We're gonna get along just fine, I can tell." Gladys nodded, then suddenly her nose twitched. "Herb, you take Brandy on to her cabin, I think my stew is burnin'." She pushed open the curtain and disappeared inside.

Herb shook his head and winked at Brandy. "She's burned the dinner for fifty-two years, but I couldn't eat it any other way." He reached into a pigeonhole and pulled out a key. "Why don't you drive down to the very last cottage and I'll meet you there."

Five minutes later Brandy was following Herb through the door of her new home. The rustic bungalow was quite a change from her luxuriously decorated duplex, but the cabin was bright and cheerful and quite spacious.

The kitchen was equipped with a full-size refrigerator, stove, double-basin sink, and ample wood-tone metal cabinets. It opened onto a dinette area that combined with a large living room. Corner windows gave the room a stunning panoramic view of the ocean and extra lighting needed to balance the dark-paneled walls. A work table had been set up under the windows and a sofa group formed a conversation area at the opposite end.

The bathroom was modern and held both a tub and shower stall. The bedroom was long and narrow with sliding glass doors that opened onto a small concrete patio. Two double dressers and an open closet area gave plenty of storage.

"You've got cable TV and a telephone," Herb told Brandy, his gaze locking onto the blank TV screen. "If you need us, just dial number one and we'll come a-runnin'."

"This is lovely." She smiled, her eyes radiating her gratitude. "I really appreciate all the extras you and Gladys added. You've made me very comfortable."

"Well, like I said, you stay with the Sullivans and you become one of the family. Gladys and me never had any kids, but we managed to keep in touch with just about everyone who's stayed with us over the last fifteen years. I've got quite a scrapbook to show off." Herb squinted at his wristwatch and grunted. "You don't mind if I get back to my ballgame. Those damn Yankees need all the fans they can get this year!"

Brandy escorted Herb to the door and watched his slow-moving figure shuffle back up the drive. She opened the rear doors of the van and proceeded to attack her own unpacking with a vengeance. By the end of two hours, Brandy was reduced to the same energy level as the aged motel manager.

The refrigerator held an ample supply of ice cubes but nothing to quench Brandy's considerable thirst or appetite. She had to settle for two glasses of water while she hastily scribbled out a grocery list. Brandy exchanged her dirty, perspiration-soaked clothes for a leotard that doubled as a swimsuit and snapped a matching teal blue skirt around her waist. Running a brush through her damp, dusty hair and slipping a pair of exercise sandals on her feet, she hurried out to the van to make a quick trip to the supermarket.

Brandy stocked up on staples—meats, fruits, and perishables—to last the week and couldn't resist a couple of bags of munchie junk food. Back at the motel, she refrigerated the perishables but left the rest of the groceries to unpack later. She felt she deserved to finally accept the Atlantic Ocean's constant invitation.

The minute her bare feet slipped into the cool frothy water Brandy felt her energy return. She stretched and inhaled deep lungfuls of bracing air. The sea had always been a tonic that never failed to refresh and revitalize.

The beach crowd had thinned as the raging high

tide made driving and parking hazardous. A tow truck was busy pulling an out-of-state vehicle free of the engine-high surf. Its driver had evidently ignored the ocean's warnings and Brandy wondered if the car would ever be driveable.

She heard a shout and looked up just in time to see a red Frisbee spiraling toward her. She jumped up, caught it, and with the flip of a wrist, sent it sailing back to its owner. Seconds later the plastic flying disc dizzily swirled back to her. Brandy found she had been included in a game by a trio of amiable bronzed and grinning young men.

The sound of her name being taken in vain jarred her concentration. The Frisbee slammed against her knuckles and fell heavily onto the ribbed wet sand. Brandy retrieved the saucer, gave it one last airborne spin, and waved a casual farewell to her unknown fellow players. Taking a deep breath, she slowly mounted the dunes not anxious to confront the griffin that waited.

Griffen St. Clair stood like a bronze obelisk against the sky. His rugged athletic physique was clothed in a white tennis outfit, his dark eyes were intense, his features hard and uncompromising. Brandy found his controlled animal energy exciting but very unpredictable. She eyed him cautiously; he looked ready to explode. *Do unto others,* she reminded herself.

"You've been in town less than three hours and already managed to acquire a male harem." Griffen sneered at her contemptuously.

Brandy gave him a demure, Mona-Lisa smile. "Thank you for such a rousing welcome. It's lovely to see you again too."

He took a deep breath, his eyes leaving her flushed face to look out at the sea. "I think we had better discuss exactly what's expected of you in the way of your behavior."

Brandy shook her head slowly, every nerve alive and ready for action. "I'm not due until tomorrow. May Day, remember?" She stepped closer to him, her fingers stroking the square angle of his jaw. "Monday morning I'll be the essence of propriety but not today."

Griffen reached to grab Brandy's shoulders, but she skillfully eluded him. His fingers tangled and clutched at the silky material of her skirt while she pirouetted to freedom. Griffen found he was left holding only her skirt, his ears ringing with the echo of her carefree laughter as he watched Brandy's lithe figure sprint into the surf.

Angrily he tossed the skirt over his shoulder and paced back and forth across the sand. The soft fabric caressed his neck; subtle tones of jasmine and roses tantalized and tormented his senses. Griffen eased down onto the sand and hurriedly reached for a cigar, hoping the imported tobacco would overpower Brandy's teasing souvenir.

The raging currents alternately pushed and pulled Brandy in crazy directions. She enjoyed playing with the forces of Neptune. It exercised her body and cleared her mind. She decided to embrace the ocean for inspiration. The sea had always been a seducer of men, lying about its temper, caressing and punishing at will. It was cunning enough to trap even the wisest sailor.

While Griffen had once again struck the first blow,

the battle had just begun. Brandy's mind plotted and schemed while she tumbled amid the cool waves. The powerful late afternoon sun pleasured her while it broiled her quarry. Then, like Venus rising from the sea, Brandy posed in the ankle-deep swirling foam. She could feel the force of Griffen's dark eyes.

Her movements were well orchestrated and deliberate. Her leotard hugged her curves like a second skin; the clinging material revealed the finer points of her femininity with blushing clarity. Instinctively Brandy knew Griffen had observed her every step. She stood in front of his seated form and wondered what was next.

Griffen inhaled a lungful of smoke and averted his gaze from Brandy's sensuous display of skin. "I hope the cold plunge in the Atlantic has rendered you a bit more sensible," came his taut rejoinder; his long fingers drilled the cigar stub into the sand.

Brandy smiled, noting with perverse satisfaction that his eyes had once again focused on the indented area of her navel. "Actually I've always found the ocean quite erotic and highly stimulating," she purred, her hands gently twisting the water from her dark hair. "I love to feel the wild rush of surf over me and the warm sun on my skin." A long luxuriant sigh escaped her full lips.

She bent from the waist to retrieve her skirt that still clung to Griffen's knit shirt. The highly visible curves of her breasts challenged his stoic expression. She saw a muscle move in his cheek and knew she had shattered his concentration.

"I hope your accommodations are satisfactory," Griffen inquired in a tightly leashed voice. He reached into his breast pocket for yet another cigar. He ruefully acknowledged that since he had met her his tobacco bill had tripled.

Brandy neatly spread her skirt on the sand and dropped down beside Griffen. "The cabin is lovely and so are the Sullivans." Her palms, derrière, and heels came in contact with the warm sand while her arms, slender torso, and long legs formed graceful arches in a typical cover-girl pose. "I love having a private stretch of beach all to myself," she told him, her chest expanding under a deep breath of salt air. "That Herb is such a pet."

"You aren't going to have time to acquire *pets,*" he retorted with heavy sarcasm. "You have six weeks to decorate four condos. That by itself is an Olympian task, but you'll also be consulting with a highly respected architectural firm on the rest of the project." Griffen's narrowed, flintlike gaze focused on her wide-eyed, attentive features. "All this work is going to have a very therapeutic effect on your overactive glands."

"Do you really think so?" Brandy queried in a fragile voice. She hoped this servile attitude wouldn't choke her. Through a thick fringe of lashes, she continued to provoke. "Sometimes I believe I'm totally beyond redemption, Griffen." She shifted her position slightly, letting her toes tangle in the laces of his Nike tennis shoes while her silken limbs casually rubbed against the hair-roughened athletic contours of his outstretched legs.

"That's nonsense!" he returned sharply, tossing his half-smoked cigar toward the lapping incoming tide. "I really believe that with a little guidance and lots of hard work, you'll come out of this a totally new woman."

"Oh, Griffen, you sound so positive." She gave a long, dramatic sigh. "I get very nervous and uptight whenever I start a new project." Her hand moved up his arm. She could feel the tense muscles expand and contract beneath her fingers.

Griffen cleared his throat. "You have no reason to be nervous." His voice had mellowed as had the forbidding expression on his lean features. "You are very talented, Brandy, and I have no doubts about your professional ability." He hadn't meant to come in contact with her body. In fact he had been steeling himself to ignore her touch. But Griffen found his hands had taken possession of her shoulders—the smooth expanse of skin was like velvet under his palms.

"I do so want you to be pleased with my work, Griffen." She took a deep breath and valiantly tried to ignore the familiar fireworks that were exploding deep within her. "I want you to be proud of the finished product. I couldn't bear to disappoint you." She leaned over him, filling his eyes with her luminous face.

"I . . . I'm sure I'll be quite satisfied," he managed in a hoarse, unsteady tone labored by ragged breathing. The hands that had meant to push her away now moved deliberately to span her waist and half-pull her into his lap.

"I want you to be pleased with me in every way." Brandy's low, hushed tones vibrated and excited him. Her breasts strained against their inadequate wet covering and branded a sensuous imprint through the thin knit of his shirt onto his heated flesh.

Griffen's firm resolve drowned in the bottomless pools of her eyes. He muttered something unintelligible and pulled her unresisting, pliant form even tighter against his virile length. Their entwined bodies melded together as remembered passions ignited the still smoldering flames of desire.

Brandy's playful tongue teased and tormented Griffen's lips. A deep growl escaped him before his mouth savagely twisted over hers. His own hard, probing tongue ached to conquer and explore the lush interior hidden behind her half-parted lips.

She spread her hands over his broad chest, letting her peach-tinted fingernails zigzag an erotic pattern over his shirt before they delicately glided up the sensitive cord of his neck to caress his jaw.

Griffen stroked the full length of her back from the nape of her neck down the supple curve of her spine. His long fingers slid easily beneath the complacent material of her swimsuit and pressed into the smooth, solid flesh of her buttocks.

The pressure on her mouth changed from domination to sharing and Brandy savored the difference. Their lips and tongues alternately aroused and satiated their mutual ardor. Her body trembled against him. She moaned softly, passions colliding under a heated rush of delicious sensations.

The unmistakable sound of musical notes accompanied the masculine hand that had captured one swelling breast. Brandy's lashes fluttered open, her diamond-bright eyes looked questioningly into Griffen's brown ones.

He cleared his throat. "My . . . my watch alarm." He shook his head to clear it. "I'm . . . I'm playing in a tennis tournament. I . . . I should be there." He stammered uncomfortably, then suddenly freed himself of her embrace.

Griffen levered himself to his feet and rubbed an unsteady hand around the back of his neck. He was at a loss to explain what had happened. After all, he was supposed to be policing her actions, not stimulating them!

Brandy gracefully rose and stood in front of him. "Good luck on your game tonight." She stretched her arms over her head. "Suddenly I'm exhausted. I think I'll turn in early. After all, tomorrow is May Day."

"Yes, May Day." Griffen cleared his throat again; his features had returned to its previous hostile expression. "I'll expect you in the office bright and early." He gave her a curt nod before striding up the dunes.

A pair of mischievous blue-gray eyes watched his tall figure disappear from sight. Moments later the sound of a car engine rudely interrupted the serenity of the desolate beach.

A soft smile curved Brandy's lips. It had been easier than she had imagined to seduce Griffen. So he thought he could tame her, did he? That man had no idea just what a relentless aggressor he was dealing with!

A little voice deep within her subconscious nagged at her moment of glory. In enticing Griffen St. Clair she ran the risk of losing control and becoming conquered by the man's potent masculine charm. She would have to carefully plan and execute her every move during the next six weeks to achieve ultimate satisfaction.

*CHAPTER SEVEN*

The morning was like chilled white wine—light, clean, and decidedly heady. Brandy embraced the day; her lungs drank in the crisp air while her eyes grew intoxicated with the view from the balcony of the penthouse at Triton Shoals.

Nature's ever-changing panorama never ceased to amaze or inspire her. The cold, expressionless, gray sky had once again become possessed by the sun. The horizon was stained with regal streaks of mauves and orchids that sent an amethyst mist rolling over the Atlantic.

Brandy leaned as far as she dared over the wrought iron railing and watched the myriad shapes that dotted the beach grow more distinct as the strengthening rays of the sun dissipated the haze. The sound of waves breaking far below on the sandy beach blended with the raucous cries of the gulls. The eastern sky was speckled with the graceful white birds and long-beaked pelicans anxious to fill their stomachs with breakfast mullet.

"When I said bright and early, I hardly meant dawn!" A deep masculine voice invaded her tranquil haven.

Brandy continued to watch the fishing birds as a smile curved her mauve-tinted lips. "I subscribe to Benjamin Franklin's theory of early to bed, et cetera." She heard Griffen's shoes crunch the concrete dust and rubble that still covered the terrace floor. "Did you win your tennis match last night?"

"As a matter of fact, I did," he announced, negligently leaning his rangy frame against the rail. His thumb and forefinger smoothed his thick mustache. "Although I was a bit off my usual game."

She cast a sidelong glance at his rugged profile. "Hmm, I thought you were in rather good form myself," came her provocative rejoinder. Brandy turned toward him. The breeze whipped her silken hair free of her face, exposing its softly rounded contours and graceful neck to the warmth of the sun. The soft folds of her sea-toned paisley dress molded against her lithe but full curves. "How did you know I was here?"

"Charlie reported to me between bites of doughnuts and mouthfuls of coffee thay my designer was already on the job." His dark eyes favored her with a decidedly sardonic gaze. "I'm surprised you had to resort to food to bribe the security guard to let you in."

Brandy laughed and stepped closer to him. The wind carried her lilting tones against his ear, then whirled them far out to sea. "I like to select my bribes to whatever a man is hungry for," her throaty voice purred. Her fingers walked up the lapels of his tan suit jacket before caressing the silken smoothness of his striped tie. "Charlie was definitely hungry for a sugary confection. How about you?" She smiled into his carved, bronzed features.

Griffen stared into her wide, luminous eyes that were more blue than smoke this morning. "I like something a bit more substantial than sweets." His voice was rough and dry.

"I thought you might," she held his brooding, half-hooded gaze for a second, then demurely lowered her dark lashes. "Although some sweets are more of a temptation than others." Her hands slowly slid free of his body.

Griffen cleared his throat and searched his pockets for his cigar case. "How long have you been here?" he inquired, clamping a thin cheroot between his even white teeth. "Have you seen the other units yet?" His large hands protectively cupped the flame on the lighter; his mouth greedily sucked in the aromatic smoke.

"Herb Sullivan walked me over about an hour ago and introduced me to the guard. Charlie is going to have to get used to having me prowl around at odd hours." Brandy smiled at his upraised brow. "I like to use natural light when I design a room. The light changes during the day and in each room."

Griffen surveyed the glowing end of his cigar then turned his attention back to Brandy. "What do you think of Triton Shoals?"

"You've got a beautiful building and beautiful units." The teasing and laughter in her voice was suddenly replaced by a serious, all-business tone. "I intend to make it even more so."

He nodded in acknowledgment of her statement. "What do you think of the penthouse?"

She moved away from the iron rail and walked through the sliding glass doors back into the living room with Griffen close behind. "Is this one yours?"

"It's replacing a house that Hurricane David decided to eliminate."

Brandy winced. "I'm sorry. Wasn't there anything left?"

He shook his head. "The only thing saved was a collection of Chinese porcelain and Southeast Asian bronze that had been on loan to the art gallery." Griffen slid one hand into his trouser pocket and gestured with the other. "You'll have free reign on this place. Just make sure it's livable and comfortable. Nothing cold or prepackaged."

"I design a house around my clients' personality. I need to know their likes and dislikes." She strolled over to the doorway that led into the huge master bedroom suite. "Their fantasies are important too." Her voice was an inviting whisper.

Griffen dropped the stub of his cigar onto the concrete subfloor and ground it out with the heel of his shoe. "I'm sure you're talented enough to handle all that on your own," he intoned dryly.

Brandy sighed and shrugged. "You've given me a mandate of very few ideas, Griffen." She mounted the three steps to the dining room and moved toward the kitchen. "I promise to do my best. I want you to be pleased."

"So you told me last night."

She flashed him a brilliant smile and picked up her purse and suede notebook from the counter. "I always keep my promises."

Griffen strode past her into the foyer and entered the waiting elevator. "The foreman of the work crew should be arriving. I'll introduce you to Ray and let him know that you're to get any help you need." His thumb jabbed the button on the panel that closed the metal doors. "You have a four o'clock appointment with Judson Stuart head of Stuart, Coleman, and Prentice, my architects."

Brandy nodded and scribbled a notation in her appointment book. "I have quite a few calls to make and people to see today."

Griffen looked at her in surprise. "I didn't realize you knew anyone in Daytona."

"An experienced designer knows the best people to get the job done in any town and any state, Mr. St. Clair," she returned evenly. Brandy's comprehensive gaze swept the bland interior of the elevator. She grimaced and shook her head. "You're going to need something in here too." More notes were scrawled in the suede book. The cover snapped closed just as the elevator doors hissed smoothly open.

The ring of heels against a concrete floor were the only sounds that echoed from the couple. Their trip through the underground parking area and return to street level was heralded by the sounds of heavy equipment warming up for a day's work.

Griffen directed Brandy toward a small mobile home that served as the construction site office. The pecan-wood paneled walls were barely visible beneath posted surveyor's maps, notice-riddled bulletin boards, and tacked-up work orders. Ray Wexler, the slim, ruddy-faced foreman, was busy checking the previous week's time cards.

After Griffen's introduction, Ray issued Brandy a security pass for her future visits. Over a cup of potent coffee, he gave her a quick summary of the work still to be completed inside the models she would be working on. Brandy listened attentively, jotted more notes in her book, and promised to send Ray a written memo of her requirements by the end of the day. By the time she and Griffen left the office, both the sun and the morning traffic had grown in strength.

Brandy eyed the sleek black Corvette for a long moment but decided to decline Griffen's stiffly formal invitation for a ride. "My office supplies are already packed," she informed him politely while she tucked her notebook in a large but neat tan satchel that doubled as her purse. "I'll just walk back to the motel and get my van."

"Van?" His large hand froze on the chrome door handle. "In Tampa you were running around in a white compact." Before Brandy could formulate a reply, Griffen's brown eyes narrowed and his mouth twisted in that all too familiar sneer. "A bed on wheels. How very appropriate!"

Brandy gave him a taut smile. Her hand came up to stroke then pat his lean cheek. "It's very convenient!" came her smug retort. She turned on her heel and briskly headed across the parking lot.

That man wasn't going to let up! Brandy roughly yanked the fallen strap of her leather bag back on her shoulder. He was always judging and condemning.

Everything was black or white to Griffen St. Clair—no shades of gray allowed!

Brandy's comely presence had not gone unnoticed by the uninformed work crew. Ordinarily she would have ignored their rather vulgar utterances. But today she decided to fight fire with fire. Griffen's sports car had yet to pass her. Why not give him something to really worry about?

She shook back her hair and took a deep breath. Brandy slowed her purposeful gait to a more leisurely, provocative stride. Her every step was enunciated by a trumpet of whistles and a stream of catcalls. Now her saintly employer would think she was ready to take on his entire construction crew!

Brandy took a few minutes to make some cosmetic repairs and brush the tangles from her shoulder-length hair. She thought about staying in the cottage longer—just to make Griffen wonder—but decided she had far too much work to get done and little enough time to do it. After all, her job was her first concern.

The offices of the St. Clair Development Company were housed a quarter mile away in a converted two-story Spanish hacienda. The red-tile-roofed, beige stucco building was surrounded by a grove of palm and cypress trees at the beginning of what looked like a restaurant row. Brandy found her employer waiting on the front steps, the ever-present cigar clamped between his teeth.

"I'm surprised you made it here alive!"

A half-smile and an arched brow was Brandy's only reply to Griffen's caustic greeting. She shifted the weight of the small corrugated carton she was holding and walked past him through the open front door into the air-conditioned office.

"Let me carry that," he ordered brusquely and tossed his black attaché case onto the brown leather sofa in the reception area.

"No, thank you," Brandy returned, her arms tightening possessively around the packing box. "If you'll just show me to my office."

Like an angry dragon, Griffen exhaled twin streams of smoke, turned, and stalked down the hallway. Brandy followed at a more sedate pace, the narrow heels of her black pumps clicking against the terrazzo floor while her eyes surveyed the perfunctory decor.

"This should make you feel right at home," Griffen commented acidly. "It was a bedroom." Despite her previous refusal of help, he wrested the carton free of her arms and set it in the center of a walnut desk.

"How thoughtful!" Brandy brushed her hands together. "Some of my most creative work has been in bedrooms." But the austere room was anything but conducive to the imagination. The walls and ceilings were painted a gray-white and old-fashioned venetian blinds hung on the only window. It looked like her first decorating challenge would be right here!

She looked at Griffen's impassive features and idly wondered if the man ever smiled. "You won't mind if I add a little pizazz to this place?"

His broad shoulders gave a careless shrug. "Be my guest. Just remember your deadline on the condos."

"I'm perfectly aware of the work involved, Mr. St.

134

Clair," she returned in a crisp, businesslike manner. "You don't have any need to worry."

A warning buzzer followed by a cheerful "good morning" echoed from the outer office. An animated, well-freckled face peered into Brandy's office. "Hi!"

"Judy Durant, this is Brandy Abbott." Griffen made the necessary introductions. "Judy is our administrative factotum." His voice had softened and a smile curved his well-shaped mouth. "Without her this whole place would fall apart."

Brandy caught her breath at the change in his tough, uncompromising features. Oh, what a smile could do! Her blue-gray eyes shifted to study the young woman who had accomplished this miracle.

Judy Durant looked barely out of her teens with a shaggy crop of auburn hair that accentuated her pert face. Her willowy, diminutive proportions made Brandy feel even more of an amazon, but the young woman's sparkling brown eyes and ever-ready smile were infectious.

"I am going to remind you of those words when my next raise is due," she joked to her boss. "It's wonderful to meet you, Brandy. I know how busy you're going to be, so if there's anyway I can help . . ."

Brandy returned her gracious smile. "Thank you. I could use a typist already." At Judy's receptive nod, she handed her five sheets of legal-size notes.

"You've done all that this morning?" Griffen's surprise registered in his voice and eyes.

Judy looked up from a cursory glance at the pages. "Brandy, what's this odd symbol that keeps being

135

repeated? And some of the words don't seem to make sense."

"I'm afraid my handwriting takes a little getting used to," she apologized, an embarrassed wave of color staining her face. "Some of my letters and words get reversed when I'm in a hurry or have a lot on my mind." Brandy smiled into Judy's puzzled face. "I have a minor form of dyslexia. Don't worry." She laughed. "It's not contagious. It's a reading and writing disability I've had since grade school."

Brandy focused on Griffen's pensive features. "It only affects the letters of the alphabet, I have no trouble with numbers and it doesn't interfere with my work. In fact I know three other dyslexic architects."

"Da Vinci, Einstein, and Woodrow Wilson were also dyslexics," he commented easily.

Her eyes widened in surprise by his knowledge. "I'm afraid I don't deserve such illustrious associates." She smiled, flushing uncomfortably under his unwavering scrutiny.

The persistent ringing of the telephone called Judy Durant back to her desk. Griffen looked at his watch. "I have outside appointments most of the morning. I'll see you at lunch."

Brandy stared at the empty doorway; a long sigh escaped her lips. Was that supposed to be an invitation? She gave a sharp shake to clear a chaotic jumble of thoughts from her mind. Her eyes rediscovered the untouched carton of office supplies.

Fifteen minutes later, Brandy was thumbing through her indispensable Roladex for the contacts she would be using on this job. By the end of an hour the telephone had become an extension of her ear. She had reacquainted herself with the East Coast suppliers and local jobbers; her appointment book was filled for the rest of the week.

She looked at the last name on her list and smiled. This was the man to start the ball rolling. She punched out his number. "Are you still aggravating your ulcer with pastrami and cream soda lunches?"

For a moment she thought the line had gone dead. Then a familiar rasping voice grated in her ear. "B. J., is that you?"

"It's me, Morris." Brandy laughed and relaxed against her brown contour desk chair. "How's the best carpet man in the business?"

"Two hundred per cent better after hearing your lovely voice," came his friendly rejoinder. "You want my carpeting in Tampa?"

"No, I want your carpeting in Triton Shoals."

Morris whistled. "Just say when, kid. Have tape measure, will travel."

"I've turned down six offers for lunch just so I could see your handsome face. How about noon at the Shoals?" Brandy stopped bantering and turned serious. "Morris, I've got to set up three condos as models and one penthouse for occupation within six weeks."

"Have I ever disappointed you, kid?" he asked, his own voice just as solemn. "I can get Sol Hanley up from Melbourne for the windows and I've got a great local mirror man." Morris paused for a moment. "My nephews are in paint and paper. You won't be sorry."

She laughed, delighted with the results. "I'll bring

enough pastrami and cream soda for everyone. See you later."

Brandy had three hours before her heartburn banquet with Morris and his associates. She left Judy Durant a list of her appointments for the week and penned a note to Griffen saying she already had a date for lunch. She could visualize his scowling reaction!

Since all the condos had patio gardens, flower boxes, and interior atriums, Brandy made arrangements to purchase the greenery—small ornamental shrubs and interior houseplants—from a local nursery. She left carrying a carton of philodendrons and ferns that would enhance her office and cottage.

After a delicatessen filled her lunch order and packed the soda in ice, Brandy returned to the Shoals. Fortunately all three of the models were on the eighth floor and the elevator made her numerous trips to the penthouse less physically taxing. She spent her time taping paint samples to the walls, studying the natural light, and developing an overall theme for each condo.

It was up to Brandy to become three different clients with unique personalities that would be reflected in each of the units. She ultimately decided that the one-bedroom condo would be in neutrals with accents in wicker and bamboo; the two-bedroom would be modern in midnight blue and silver, glass, and chrome accessories; the three-bedroom would reflect the serenity and tranquility of the Orient.

Griffen's penthouse—well, since he was letting her make all the decisions—that would of necessity be

138

eclectic, with an emphasis on form, color, and textures. She would make sure the furnishings could be exchanged to suit his preference.

"B. J., I smell the pastrami," a booming voice echoed through the eighth-floor hallway and into the open doors. "Where the hell are you?"

"Straight ahead, Morris." Brandy caroled cheerfully. "Just follow your nose."

The nose, a pair of vibrant blue eyes, and a sun-weathered face peered around the foyer door and spied Brandy standing in the center of a sunken living room. "Hey, kid, you haven't changed since the Kirkland job." Morris Reno's rangy figure sauntered into the room.

"The Kirkland job made us all twenty years older," Brandy returned dryly. She smiled at him, then found herself wrapped in his arms, his bald head coming to the tip of her nose. "It's good to see you again, Morris. How's Betty and the kids?"

"Why do you mention my wife and family every time I get your gorgeous body in a clinch?" He moaned, gave her one final squeeze, and grinned at her. "Everyone is fine. I just bundled my last off to college." Morris's keen eyes darted around the interior of the apartment. "So this is what you're going to transform into a palatial delight worthy of its kingly price tag."

"This and three more like it," she announced, gesturing for him to look around. "Where's Sol and the others?"

"Right here!" sang another familiar voice from the doorway. Sol Hanley, the reed-thin, perpetually

139

smiling drapery man gave Brandy a bear hug. "It's nice to work with you again, B. J."

He introduced her to Steve Halley, a dark-haired rather intense man in his mid-thirties who Sol proclaimed was an artist with mirrors and stained glass.

Brandy blinked uncertainly at Morris's blond nephews, Sam and Matt. The twin Adonises were in their early twenties and looked more like sun-bronzed beach boys than the promised painters and wallpaper experts.

"Don't worry about those two." Sol winked and gave Brandy's hand a reassuring pat as they trailed the others into the living room. "Those boys do work as beautiful as they look!"

Lunch turned into a roving meal. Brandy led her associates on a tour of the three models and the penthouse. She outlined her plans while they studied the various interiors. Suggestions and changes were bantered back and forth.

Then they went back and dissected each unit. Sol took window measurements; Morris sketched the rooms for carpeting and noted the colors; the twins went over the walls and indicated what would be needed to prep them for paint and paper; and Steve conferred with Brandy on the use of mirrors for various accents.

Two hours later they had reassembled in the living room of the penthouse. "Well, gentlemen—" Brandy settled onto a folding chair, her ever-present notebook open on her knees "—let's hear all the problems." She leveled a questioning gaze toward Sam and Matt.

The young men favored her with blinding twin

smiles. It was Matt who spoke. "We'll be here at seven tomorrow to size the walls for paper. You phone us the paint colors and we can have the job done by Monday."

She nodded her satisfaction. "Morris?"

He licked his thumb, then riffled through his notes. "I've got the pearl gray, the dark blue, the brown, and the buff tweed in stock. You want a little artistry in the single with the sunken living room, no problem. You'll have to come to the store and pick out the Oriental accent you want for in here." Morris peered at her over the tops of his reading glasses. "When the boys get through painting, we lay the carpet. Give me an extra day here and there, but you're talking next Friday complete."

"As always, you make life very easy for me." Brandy flashed him a grateful smile. "Sol, how does it look from your end?"

"I'm afraid I'm not going to be so easy." He scratched the back of his neck while he did some refiguring. Sol looked at her and shook his head. "Even though you've kept things simple, we're looking at three weeks minimum. I have the bamboo blinds in stock, but the shades and shutters will have to be ordered, likewise the vertical blinds. The cornices and lambrequins have to be cut and fabricked." Sol sent her an apologetic glance. "Sorry, Brandy."

"That's okay. We've got time to play with." She turned her attention to Steve. "What about the mirror work?"

"I've got a warehouse full of ceiling squares. The closet panels will take a week to get and I'd like another two weeks to do that hand etching for the dining room wall grouping." Steve's intense features gave way to a half-smile. "I'm really going to enjoy this, I never get anything more exciting than a mirrored bedroom ceiling."

"We'll see how much he enjoys this when B. J. starts cracking her whip," Morris's raspy voice interceded. "She made my marine sergeant sound like my grandmother!"

Brandy's tongue clicked against the roof of her mouth. "Shame on you, Morris, for casting aspersions on my charm. I don't ever remember you or Sol threatening a mutiny."

Sol raised his ragged gray brows and grinned at her. "We did, however, discuss various evil tortures to your nubile body."

Griffen St. Clair's deep voice sliced through the laughter that vibrated around the room. "Strange, but those were my exact thoughts today when my designer didn't show up for lunch."

Brandy cast a cool, backward glance over her shoulder. "I'm afraid the temptation of having lunch with five men was just a pleasure I couldn't resist." She favored her employer with a dazzling smile. Brandy stood and introduced him to her colleagues.

Griffen tapped his gold digital watch. "You are also in danger of being late for your four o'clock appointment," he reminded her.

She gave a low groan of remembrance and hastily checked through her notes. "I think we're all through. Morris, I'll be in on Thursday. Steve, you can start next Wednesday, and, Matt and Sam, I'll see you tomorrow."

When the elevator doors closed on the departing

142

men, Griffen directed an inquiring stare at Brandy. "You certainly put an army together fast, especially for someone who's never worked in Daytona before."

Brandy packed her notebook in her tan satchel. "Morris, Sol, and I carpeted, draped, and decorated six homes in the Keys during the last two years," she informed him in a controlled voice. "We meshed from the first. Their work is the best and so are their products. It makes life easier, especially when the timetable is this tight."

She took a deep breath, smoothed her hands against the soft jersey skirt of her dress, and stood tall and stately in front of Griffen. "I hope my every move is not going to be subjected to an interrogation. You said free reign and no hassles. I expect you to keep your word."

Griffen folded his arms across his massive chest and rocked back and forth on the heels of his shoes. "I expect you to keep your part of the bargain and concentrate all your energies on your work." His gaze roamed over her feminine proportions. "I saw the way the two boys from muscle beach were eyeing your nubile body," he cracked sarcastically.

A bubble of laughter escaped Brandy's lips. "Why, Griffen—" she stepped closer to him, her diamond-bright eyes teasing his granite-hard features "—blond beach boys do nothing for my libido."

Her long fingers ruffled the vibrant coils of hair at his temple. "I prefer dark-haired—" her hand caressed his cheek "—square-jawed—" her thumb and forefinger smoothed his mustache and pulled down his lower lip "—tough-looking brutes."

She felt his hand lock into her waist; her eyes never left his. When his mouth lowered, Brandy gave a little sigh and broke free of his embrace. "But, then, I did promise to behave." She tapped his watch. "Look at the time, we better get moving!"

The Brandy Abbott that walked into the architectural offices of Stuart, Coleman, and Prentice was the consummate businesswoman. Her hair and makeup were neat and understated, an expertly tailored navy blazer had turned her soft dress into a uniform, and her attitude was crisp and professional.

It gave Griffen St. Clair cause to wonder if he wasn't losing his mind! How could she be a teasing temptress one minute and an efficient executive the next? What annoyed him the most was the fact that he so easily succumbed to both of them!

Judson Stuart reminded Brandy of her father. They both were tall, broad-shouldered, and gray-haired. Their glacier eyes could freeze the equator. She doubted a smile had ever upturned Mr. Stuart's austere mouth. After Griffen's introduction, Brandy extended her hand and received a punishing grip in return. This was not going to be an easy interview.

"Well, Miss Abbott, you seem to have done the impossible and pleased Mr. St. Clair," Judson Stuart intoned dryly. He leaned back in his leather chair, his sharp eyes focused on Brandy's youthful appearance. "I spoke to Henry Braddock about you."

She hastily swallowed the lump that threatened to strangle her vocal cords. "How is Professor Braddock?"

"Fine. He told me you were one of his brightest students."

She smiled slightly. Her moist palms relaxed their death grip on the arms of the chair. "For a woman, he probably added."

Judson arched a dark brow; his mouth twisted in a wry grin. "Actually he said you were bright, talented, sharp, and annoyingly persistent. I hope you haven't changed."

Brandy's thumb twisted the zodiac signet ring on her little finger. "I'm afraid those qualities are ingrained, sir."

His keen eyes studied her for a moment, then he pulled his leather appointment calendar into the center of his oak desk. "I know you have a design project to complete in six weeks." He flipped the pages then reached for his desk pen. "I'll expect you to start your internship with us on June twenty-fifth."

Startled, Brandy blinked at him. "Thank you."

"You won't be thanking me, Miss Abbott," he returned evenly. "You'll work harder than ever with no time to call your own." Judson's voice softened slightly. "Perhaps we will also learn from you; your solar plans are very comprehensive. Of course your designs will be on the drawing board for eighteen months and some of your specs are very idealistic."

Brandy's heart jammed painfully against her ribs. She knew she should nod and smile and shut up, but once again she ignored her sensible instincts. "What did you feel was so impractical, sir?"

Judson Stuart pressed the tips of his fingers together. The iciness of his gaze and the coolness of his voice strove to intimidate. "*Two* that come to mind are your wall structures and insulation depth."

Brandy cleared her throat and made her tone as congenial as possible. "Walls should be able to withstand at least seventy-mile-per-hour winds in Florida. I've seen paint peeled off in less." She licked her lips and continued, despite the feeling of dread that had invaded her system. "I also feel that using such a high R value in insulating walls and ceilings will make a house more energy efficient."

"We've discussed this before, Judson." Griffen's powerful voice took control of the conversation. "The cost to us is minimal compared to what the consumer will save."

"I try to keep all your costs minimal and your profits high, Griffen," the older man returned evenly. His gaze shifted once again to Brandy. "I can see you are still annoyingly persistent in your ideas, Miss Abbott."

"I'm afraid so, Mr. Stuart." Her next words were offered with obvious reluctance and a dread of acceptance. "Perhaps you would like to rescind your internship?"

"No, as I said before, we can all learn." Judson Stuart turned his attention back to Griffen but Brandy heard little of their conversation. There was no doubt in her mind her internship with Stuart, Coleman, and Prentice would enhance her knowledge and inspire her creativity, but it would also exhaust her self-control. She found the dichotomies exhilarating!

Griffen's large hand filled the small of Brandy's back as he guided her toward her parked van. "Congratulations." He paused then cast her a sidelong glance. "Would you like to go out and celebrate?"

Brandy looked at him in surprise. Was he testing her again? This time she decided to tell the truth. "No, thank you, Griffen. My only celebration will be a long soak in a tub of hot, scented water and a bowl of corn flakes." She yanked open the driver's door. "I still have a lot of work to do tonight."

A self-satisfied smile twisted his features. "You see, I told you hard work was just what you needed to keep you on the straight and narrow."

She gave him a smug smile of her own and squeezed the well-developed biceps of his right arm. "I'll get my second wind in a few days. I hate sleeping single in a double bed."

She climbed into the van, slammed the door, and gunned the engine to life. That should entertain his thoughts for tonight!

## CHAPTER EIGHT

Griffen rocked back against his brown executive chair, his dark eyes inspecting the fresh coat of paprika-colored paint that had transformed the dull walls of his office. Brandy had been right, he conceded diffidently—the odd shade he had balked at using was somehow quite soothing.

He contemplated the other changes she had made. Elegant woven wood shades graced the windows, framed prints enhanced the walls, and hanging baskets of ferns brought life to unused corners. During the last four weeks Brandy's decorating artistry had not only worked magic in the sterile condo units but had swept his office as well.

Brandy had been putting in sixteen-hour days. He should know—he had dogged her every step! Griffen stared at the stucco ceiling, his mouth twisting in wry self-derision. At first he had been monitoring her behavior, watching and waiting for just one slip. But

Brandy had been all work and no play. She was up at dawn to instruct the workers, dashing around the city buying and ordering during the day, then back at the Shoals at dusk to check on progress and handle any problems.

While the workmen plied their trades in the models, Brandy had taken control of the penthouse herself. Griffen had discovered her secret evening rendezvous with paint and wallpaper. He had also discovered another Brandy Abbott. This one wore pigtails, a disreputable pair of cutoffs and a T-shirt spangled with shades of latex and gluey paste. This one sang off key while she expertly painted walls and hung paper.

He had become exhausted just keeping track of her schedule; he could well imagine how physically taxed Brandy was, living that grueling pace. He no longer worried about her morals—only about her health!

Griffen closed his eyes, his mind drifting back to the night he had stopped at her motel to leave the signed purchase orders she needed for early the next morning. Although the cabin was ablaze with lights, Brandy failed to answer his knock. He peered through the window and saw her slumped across a drafting table. Expecting the worst, Griffen shouldered his way into the cottage, but when he heard her telltale snores, he realized she had merely fallen asleep.

"I should never have taken that bath," Brandy yawned, struggling to unglue her leaden eyelids. "Could you make me some coffee, I really have to—"

"You really have to go to bed," he snapped gruffly.

Ignoring her mumbled protests, Griffen pulled her limp body from the chair, his sinewy arms quick to support her rag-doll anatomy. "You can work on this tomorrow."

"It was supposed to be done last week," she murmured against his shoulder. "I can't keep telling the editor of *Handyman* magazine that it's in the mail."

"If he calls again, refer him to me. I'll handle everything," he promised, half-pushing half-pulling her lassitude-impaired body into the moonlit bedroom.

Yanking back the bedcovers, Griffen turned his attention back to Brandy, who appeared to have fallen asleep on her feet. "And you wanted to keep working!" He grunted, shook his head in amazement, and untied the belt of her white kimono.

His hands slid beneath the silken fabric, easing it free of her shoulders and arms. Brandy stood before him in a silly piece of feminine frippery that didn't quite reach her knees. The muted light illuminated the sensuous curves the wispy nightgown vainly tried to conceal.

She yawned and sniffed. "Maybe I'll just take a little nap. Set the alarm and—"

Griffen's fingers bit into the soft skin of her shoulders and gave her an impatient shake. Her eyes flew open. "You are going to get a full eight hours." He enunciated each word as if he were dealing with a recalcitrant child.

Then both his voice and his features softened. "Brandy, take it a little easier." His fingers threaded through the silken tumble of her amber hair. "You're

150

way ahead of schedule. You don't need to kill yourself."

She blinked at him, her lips curving into a sleepy smile. "But I want everything perfect. I want you to be—"

"Pleased." Griffen exhaled a heavy sign. "I am pleased, very pleased." His brooding dark gaze was hypnotized by the shimmering liquid pools of her eyes. A helpless groan escaped his throat. Griffen lowered his head, his probing tongue and firm mouth anxiously plundering her softly parted lips.

His hands roamed possessively over the hills and valleys of her feminine silhouette. The slippery sheer nightgown and the creamy expanse of skin aroused his desires and fed his frustrations. He wanted to go on kissing and caressing her, to hold her in his arms all night, to make sure she slept and then in the morning he wanted . . .

Angrily he shook his head, thrusting the carnal memories away. What the hell was the matter with him? Brandy had monopolized his thoughts since their first encounter in Tampa. He knew what she was—that should have made her all the easier to forget.

Was. Maybe that's the key. Lately Brandy had been different, more relaxed, more friendly, more at ease. Perhaps all the hard work had reformed her.

He pushed himself out of the chair, walked to the window, and stared with unseeing eyes at the swaying palm trees. Brandy was doing a magnificent job. Why was he so damn reluctant to praise her? Maybe they could start over again, get to know each other.

Griffen looked at his watch and smiled. Why not take her to lunch?

The door of Brandy's office was half open. Griffen saw her long, sleek legs, crossed at the ankles, on the corner of the desk. Her melodic voice carried out into the hallway.

"Dee, I am a desperate woman. Four weeks! I have never been so frustrated." Startled, Griffen silently inched closer. He heard her groan. "Believe me, I have looked, but only you have what I need. Send me Pierre."

Her husky laugh grated against his ears. His fingers fell away from the doorknob, his hands curled into fists. "Of course I realize how big he is. Believe me, he's just what I need. And I need him fast. Put him on the shuttle and I'll pick him up at the airport tomorrow." He heard her laugh again. "I know. I can just imagine what everyone will say. Do you think I care? Having Pierre will make anything bearable."

Griffen quietly backed down the hall to his office. He leaned against the closed door, his chest rising and falling under an invisible weight. How could he have been so stupid to think Brandy had changed!

He cracked each knuckle of his hands. Changed! My God she was worse! Now she was ordering a man the way she ordered furniture!

Well, enough was enough. He was going to put a stop to this right now! Griffen's long legs ate up the hallway. He flung open her door, only to be confronted by an empty office. "Judy," he yelled, striding purposefully into the reception area. "Where did Brandy go?"

Judy blinked at her employer's tightly leashed features. "She ran across the street for lunch. She's got a heavy schedule this after—"

He didn't wait to hear the rest. Griffen bolted from the building and sprinted across the four-lane highway; bleating car horns and squealing tires accompanied his every step.

Brandy's tall figure, clad in a jade green blouse and pewter skirt, was easily discernible among the casually dressed, mostly elderly crowd standing in line for the smorgasbord. Muttering vague words of apology, Griffen inched his way to her side. "I want to talk to you."

Brandy smiled and passed him a tray and a plate. "This is a nice surprise."

"I'm the one surprised or, more precisely, fooled." His low savage tone had her blinking. "I thought you had changed, but I guess they're right when they say you can't teach an old dog new tricks."

Brandy calmly replaced the tongs in the salad bowl and silently chanted her mantra. "I have no idea what you are talking about."

Griffen dropped a haphazard collection of greens onto his dish. "Please don't expect that wide-eyed innocent look to work on me. I know all about Pierre." His harsh tones overruled her sputtered explanation. "I consider myself fairly liberal-minded, but what . . . what you're doing is disgusting and illegal. Really, Brandy, I never thought you'd sink low enough to call a male prostitute."

The elderly, blue-haired lady next to Griffen lost her hold on the cottage-cheese spoon. It clattered to the floor, sending a shower of white curds against her seersucker culottes.

Brandy took a deep, controlling breath and resisted the urge to dump her tray on Griffen's head. She licked her lips and cleared her throat; her words were aimed at his jugular. "We are two consenting adults, Griffen. It is the world's oldest profession." She added a collection of raw vegetables to her plate. "Women have been servicing men for years. Now, men, like Pierre, are providing the same service for us. There are male strippers; why not male hookers?" She cast him a sardonic glance. "I can even use my MasterCard or Visa."

The balding, septuagenarian at Brandy's right elbow fumbled with the soup ladle and ended up with a shirt cuff drenched in clam chowder.

"I don't understand you," Griffen ground out through clenched teeth. "You seem perfectly normal." He picked up a meat fork, jabbed at the slices of roast beef, and slammed them onto his dish. "Maybe you need professional help."

Brandy smiled at him, her tone one of patient forbearance. "Actually I'm a product of my environment." She picked up a rolled linen napkin containing silverware, moved out of line, and headed toward a private table in the corner of the large dining room.

Her emotions ranged from deadly calm to seething turmoil. No matter what she said or what she did, that insufferable man would see only what he wanted. And he so wanted a nymphomaniac!

"What the hell do you mean, you're a product of your environment?" Griffen slid into the chair next to her. "For the last four weeks your environment

154

has been filled with hard work. If anything—" his dark eyes cast a searing glance at her controlled, poised features "—you should be too exhausted to even think of entertaining Pierre."

Brandy exhaled an airy, musical sigh. "What you have to realize, Griffen, is that my whole world revolves around sensuality." Her long fingers stroked the slender column of throat down to the low V of her neckline. "Interior designing and architecture are very erotic occupations." She picked up a carrot stick, studied it for a moment, then placed it in her mouth, her teeth snapped off the end. "Phallic symbols abound—look at the skyscrapers, chimneys, polelamps, and all those groin vaults."

A lazy smile curved Brandy's lips; she watched his skin turn gray beneath his tan. "And, Griffen, what about geodesic domes?" She reached for a Spanish olive. Her tongue circled its green skin several times before poking out the red pimiento. "They are very mammary-oriented in their design." Brandy leaned forward, staring intently into his glazed eyes. "Now tell me the truth, Griffen—" her finger zigzagged along the curve of his cheekbone to the edge of his tight, compressed mouth "—don't you lust in your heart every time you drive through a tunnel?"

"Erotic symbolism is everywhere." Brandy studied his tray, then picked up her fork. "Just look at your lunch." She neatened the blob of cottage cheese on his dish and centered the cherry. "And doesn't that sausage look right at home snuggled between those two halves of baked potato."

"Griffen." Her voice was low and infinitely inviting. "Women have needs and those needs have to be

155

answered." Brandy eased her right foot free of her gray pump. Her stockinged toes crawled up his shoes, under the leg opening of his trousers, then proceeded to nuzzle and caress the tensed muscles of his calf. "I would have never had to put in that call to Pierre if you hadn't been so stingy."

Her hand slid beneath the table, her fingers clamped onto his knee. Griffen's body stiffened, but Brandy refused to acknowledge the silent protest. Her hand moved slowly up the sensitive length of his inner thigh, her palm and fingers aimlessly stroking upward toward his belt buckle. "You've frustrated me at every turn," Brandy told him, her eyes hungrily devouring his impassive features. "What else was I to do?"

Griffen cleared his throat and reached inside his navy blazer, fumbling for his cigar case. Brandy's hand closed over his breast pocket. "Sorry, darling." She patted his lapel. "This is the no-smoking section." She slid her foot back into her shoe. "You know, you really should try to quit," she told him seriously. "There's a definite link between smoking and impotency, especially in men of your age." Her dark lashes fluttered flirtatiously. "I'd hate for that to happen to you."

Brandy looked at the wall clock and sighed. "Oh, dear, I really have to cut lunch short. I have an afternoon crammed full of appointments." She leaned over and put her warm mouth against his thin lips. "Enjoy your lunch, darling."

Judy Durant was just putting the vinyl cover over her electric typewriter when her boss literally staggered in the front door. At first she thought Griffen was drunk. But after a more thorough examination she realized his lack of agility was due to exhaustion. "It would have been nice if you called, Griffen. I lied your way out of three appointments and there's a stack of phone messages on your desk." She arched a copper brow and stared at him. "What have you been doing?"

He slumped into a chair, his dark head cupped between his hands. "I'm sorry, I know I should have called." Griffen looked up at her, his mouth twisted in a humorless grin. "I spent the afternoon beating my frustrations on the racquetball court."

Judy folded her arms across her chest. "Griffen, I've been working with you for the last year and I thought I really understood you. But lately—" she shook her neat cap of red hair and frowned at him "—I just can't understand. I do know it has something to do with Brandy."

Griffen winced. His fingers raked through his shower-damp hair. "I don't suppose she's back."

"No." Judy pulled open a black metal file drawer and reached for her straw purse. "If you do see Brandy, please tell her there's a phone message on her desk and Pierre arrived a day early."

"What!" Griffen's head snapped up, his brown eyes radiating angry fire. "Pierre is here, in this office?"

Judy nodded. "I got a call from the airport and went out to pick him up." Her freckled face broke into a wide smile. "I can see why Brandy was all excited. He's darling."

He lunged to his feet and slammed his fist into his

palm. "I can't believe she had the nerve to have him come here." He exhaled forceably. "I'm really sorry that you had to get involved in this."

"Oh, I didn't mind," she told him airily, then burst into a fit of giggles. "He did cause a few heads to turn. I don't envy Brandy coping with him." Judy pursed her lips thoughtfully. "I really think I'm going to order Joey, he's not as big as Pierre, but then—"

"For God's sake, Judy," Griffen interrupted harshly, "I can't believe that you're getting involved with this. I thought you were going with Bill."

She looked at him, her forehead creasing in puzzlement. "Why should Bill mind?" Judy shrugged, completely mystified. "I suppose it is a little avantgarde."

"That's putting it mildly," he retorted in a rude tone. Griffen paced back and forth across the entry foyer. "What did you tell Pierre?"

"Tell Pierre?" Judy's confused eyes followed the agitated action of her employer. "What are you talking about?"

"Well, the man certainly can't spend the night here." Griffen took a deep breath. "I suppose it's up to me to handle this." He strode down the corridor to Brandy's office, knocked once, then pushed the door open.

His eyes widened at the sight of Pierre. He walked in and slowly circled the desk, shaking his head in disbelief. Pierre was a three-foot high, porcelain pelican, white wings outstretched in flight.

"Isn't he darling?" Judy's voice chirped from the doorway. She unfolded a color brochure on the desk.

"I'm ordering Joey." She pointed to a smaller pelican, his head cocked at a rakish angle, sitting on wood pilings. "He'll be perfect for the garden in the back of my apartment."

"You . . . you made him sound like a person." Griffen stammered stupidly. He took a deep breath and shook his head. "I thought Pierre was a man."

"Well, you do begin to believe the birds are human." Judy pushed the pamphlet toward Griffen. "Each bird has its own name, special personality traits, it's a cute idea—the Pelican Adoption Agency."

Griffen wearily rubbed his forehead. He stared at the pelican, the bird's blue eyes and gaping beak seemed to be laughing at his disorientation. "I thought . . . I thought Brandy had ordered . . ." His voice trailed off.

Judy sighed. "You aren't making much sense. I think all that handball must have addled your brain." She turned and started for the door. "By the way, I managed to get you a ticket on the red-eye flight to San Francisco. It leaves Daytona at midnight and you'll be back early Tuesday." Judy checked her watch. "I've got to get going. Bill is taking me out for our usual Friday night dinner and a movie." She called over her shoulder. "If you see Brandy, tell her that Tony phoned. I know she's been trying to reach her brother all morning."

Griffen blinked. "Tony Cameron in Tampa?"

"Hmm." Judy nodded. "I think it's lovely the way Brandy and her brother have such a close relationship. My brothers and I fight all the time." She

159

smiled at him. "Have a nice evening and don't miss your plane."

Griffen replaced the receiver of the telephone and leaned back in Brandy's desk chair. So Tony *was* really her half-brother; her father was the commissioner of police in Palm Beach; and Pierre—Griffen's brown eyes surveyed his stalwart companion—Pierre turned out to be made of stone.

A deep growl of laughter erupted from his throat. He rubbed his square jaw and shrewdly eyed the pelican. "Pierre, she may have us in check, but, we aren't checkmated." Griffen stood up and patted the bird's head. "I think it's time Brandy Abbott was taught a lesson."

His laughing expression changed to one of devilish enthusiasm. "I've got six hours before my plane leaves; let's just see how much heat that designing woman can handle!"

## CHAPTER NINE

"Good evening."

The tune Brandy was humming lodged sideways in her throat. "How . . . how did you get in?" she stammered, her eyes registering her surprise at finding the supine form of Griffen St. Clair ensconced on her sofa.

He smiled, watching while she struggled to get the key free of the lock. "Herb Sullivan. You're right, he is a pet." Griffen glanced pointedly at his watch. "I was getting worried, it's almost seven."

"I think I mentioned that I had a very heavy schedule today." Her words were uttered with caution. She didn't like the way Griffen was staring at her or the way he smiled and showed all thirty-two teeth. She had seen that same expression on a barracuda in a tank at Sea World just before it had devoured another fish.

Brandy laid her tan purse and shopping bag on the

dinette table and walked slowly toward Griffen's reclining figure. "Was there something you wanted?"

He grinned again and stroked his mustache, his dark eyes feasting on her feminine attributes. "I'm taking you out for a farewell dinner."

Her shoulders sagged. "You're . . . I'm . . . fired?"

"Don't be silly." Griffen quickly vaulted to his feet. "You know how pleased I am with your work." His white teeth contrasted with the deep bronze of his rugged features.

Brandy folded her arms protectively across her breasts; her blue-gray eyes shrewdly sized up his inordinately happy expression. "I don't quite understand."

He brushed an infinitesimal speck of lint from the sleeve of his black suit, adjusted the neck of his pearl-gray shirt, and straightened his tie. "I'm leaving on the midnight flight for a three-day trip to California." His dark gaze meshed with hers. "And I can't think of anyone I'd rather spend the next four hours with than you."

Griffen's virile fingers curved around Brandy's jade-green silk-covered shoulders. "I took the liberty of picking out your dress for the evening." His deep voice reached out to erase her unspoken qualms. "It's right on your bed." He gave her a little push in that direction. "Hurry up, darling, our reservations are in thirty minutes."

Brandy paced up and down in front of her dresser. Something was definitely wrong! Her eyes nervously darted back and forth from the locked bedroom door to the anxious face reflected in the mirror.

What had happened to the shell-shocked man she

had left in the restaurant at noon? That Griffen St. Clair she could handle but this . . . this new, very in-control Griffen would need a whip and a chair! His animal energy and inherent masculine charm was directed at one person—her!

A shiver of pure physical awareness coursed down Brandy's spine. She knew how attracted she was to Griffen when he was at his arrogant best. Would she be able to resist this man whose husky voice and passion-filled eyes caressed her like fingers? Did she want to resist?

Brandy collapsed on the edge of the bed, her mind a chaotic jumble of turbulent questions and no answers. Her distraught gaze was snagged by the black handkerchief-skirted dress that was centered on the blue chenille spread. The slinky fabric and the flirtatious plunging neckline promised a lot more than Brandy ever expected to deliver.

She closed her eyes and took five deep breaths. She would not lose control. Her mouth twisted in a rueful grin. This must have been exactly what Dr. Frankenstein said when he discovered his monster had gotten loose.

Brandy pulled her blouse over her head and unbuttoned her skirt. There were many ways a woman could keep a man in line and she only had to restrain Griffen until midnight. The witching hour—how appropriate!

King Arthur's restaurant on the twenty-ninth floor of the Peck Plaza provided an enchanting view of an unforgettable sunset on the Atlantic Ocean. The early evening sky was stained in a rhapsody of crimsons and golds. Rainbow-sailed catamarans skimmed over the glittering, glasslike surf.

Brandy took her eighteenth sip of Dom Pérignon and searched the recesses of her mind for something clever to say. She had already discussed the awe-inspiring view, the beautiful weather, the progress on the condos and, quite frankly, she was exhausted. One-sided conversations always had a tendency to do that.

Her fingers straightened the amber candle arrangement while her blue-gray eyes surreptitiously studied Griffen from beneath a fringe of sooty lashes. So far he had been the epitome of puritanical chivalry. But Brandy wasn't fooled! The evening had a nerve-frazzling cloud of premeditation hanging over it.

A bottle of precisely chilled champagne waited expectantly in a silver ice bucket, a sartorially perfect waiter kept her crystal goblet filled to the brim, and the nuisance of ordering seemed to have been eliminated. Nothing as vulgar as a menu invaded their intimate window booth, but a seafood appetizer, replete with oysters, shrimp, and scallops had been delivered and consumed.

Perhaps the one thing that unnerved Brandy the most was the fact that for the last hour Griffen hadn't smoked one cigar! He was smiling and relaxed and inordinately carefree. It made her feel the need for a smoke!

Brandy was relieved when the waiter reappeared. She wouldn't be expected to both talk and eat. She gazed in surprise at the contents of the silver serving dish—she had been expecting a salad, not this rather unusual assortment of vegetables. She gave a mental shrug and selected wine-soaked chestnuts, cherry tomatoes, olives, and a caviar-anointed hard-boiled egg.

Griffen smiled and slid an artichoke onto his salad plate. "I have been very inconsiderate toward you and I'd like to apologize."

Brandy swallowed the olive, blotted her lips, and eyed his enigmatic expression cautiously. "I'm afraid I don't understand."

"I've been doing a lot of soul-searching since our conversation this noon." He pulled off one petal of the artichoke and dipped it into the lemon butter. "I think it was rather presumptuous of me to expect you to turn your life around so quickly."

She watched his even white teeth scrape away at the tender flesh. "I'm sure you were just doing what you thought was right," Brandy returned quickly, her voice sounding oddly high.

"But what's right for one person is not necessarily right for another," Griffen countered smoothly. His large hand imprisoned hers against the pristine white tablecloth. His thumb made tiny circles against the underside of her wrist. He could feel her pulse jump beneath his finger.

Brandy vainly tried to ignore the little impulses that shook her arm. "I'm sure I'll straighten out eventually." She laughed with reckless abandon. "All this work keeps me very busy."

"It really is a shame that your choice of a career fans the fires, so to speak." Griffen answered the silent question emanating from Brandy's eyes. "As you told me this afternoon, architecture is highly erotic. I know how a frustration can become an obsession."

She moistened her apricot-tinted lips with her tongue as her body wriggled uncomfortably against the black velvet chair cushion. "Griffen." Brandy cleared her throat but found her words obstructed by a cherry tomato that he placed between her teeth.

"Have a love apple, darling." His husky, low-pitched voice stroked her high-strung demeanor. "In fact I've ordered a banquet of love just for us."

The small cherry tomato was swallowed whole. "You . . . you did?"

Griffen nodded. "We started with Casanova's favorite dish—oysters. Then this rather sensuous array of vitamin-packed vegetables." His smooth forehead puckered thoughtfully. "Of course the caviar should be eaten in bed."

He sighed and shrugged his broad shoulders. "The pièce de résistance is Tornedo Rossini, the choicest cut of beef with erotic glamour of foie gras and truffles."

He pointedly ignored Brandy's stunned features, his virile fingers entwined with hers. "I don't want you to rely on the likes of a man like Pierre to satisfy your needs and desires." His eyes burned with the promise of an evening of passion. "You're right, darling, I have been stingy but tonight . . ." Griffen lifted Brandy's hand and pressed his warm lips into her palm. His tongue and teeth teased the fleshy mound near her thumb. "Tonight is ours."

The meal was relaxed and unrushed, but only Griffen savored each morsel. Brandy managed to choke down the gourmet cuisine only under his persistent encouragement and a substantial quantity of champagne. The expensive, potent wine was the only thing that made the evening palatable.

The slow, sensual strains of music from the restaurant's combo drifted into their intimate world of two. Griffen pulled Brandy to her feet and swung her onto the dance floor, their bodies melting together in perfect synchronization.

This was the first time Brandy ever regretted her choice of shoes. The high-heeled black evening sandals that usually intimidated added the extra few inches needed to put her eyes and mouth almost on level with Griffen's.

He eagerly made the most of the situation. His lips roamed along the rounded contours of her flushed cheeks; his tongue teasingly circled the diamond stud in her ear lobe. "Your perfume haunts me like a passion." The low growl that escaped his throat caused her to jump.

"Griffen." Brandy gasped and tried to shrink free of his captive embrace. "If you hold me any closer, I'll be in back of you."

His deep chuckle vibrated in her shell-like ear. "Darling, you have such an adorable sense of humor." Griffen moved his head, his dark gaze instantly hypnotized by her lambent silvery eyes. "You also have the most inviting mouth and the most glorious hair."

Fun and games turned into desire, desire that was no longer hidden but fastened to his prey. Griffen rained kisses on her full lips, her pert nose, and her delicate eyelids. His capable hands sculpted her lush curves tight against his rugged length.

A submissive sigh escaped Brandy. She burrowed her cheek into the curved hollow of Griffen's neck. She had meant to keep her wits about her; she had meant to challenge his every move, his every word. But the man who held her, whose very touch aroused a fever that raged through her, had ceased to be a predator. The crisp, clean scent of his cologne inflamed her senses and her heart throbbed in a frantic rhythm that contrasted with the melody coming from the orchestra.

Blame it on a dinner of aphrodisiacs, a magnum of champagne, the soft lights, and the romantic surroundings, but Brandy didn't demur when Griffen whispered it was time to go.

A silent silvery moon had replaced the red sun in a dark blue sky dazzled with stars. A balmy ocean breeze filtered through the Corvette's open windows as Griffen piloted the sports car along the beach drive.

It had been a wonderfully romantic evening. Brandy settled back against the white leather bucket seat, her eyes silently condemning the gear box that kept her from snuggling close to Griffen's rugged body.

A rush of excitement sent a heated tide washing over her skin. In a few more miles they would be at her motel and their love banquet would continue with, as Griffen had teasingly put it, dessert.

Brandy glanced over at him. He was totally preoccupied with driving, trying to keep the low-slung sports car from spinning out in the soft sand. The green glow of the dashboard lights brought out the harsh planes and angles of Griffen's face. Brandy swallowed and fidgeted uncomfortably; she recognized the expression that twisted his tough features —she had seen it whenever he criticized her behavior.

What had happened to the saint who was bent on reforming her? This man seemed anxious to feast on her presumed needs. Doubt grew stronger and kept nagging at Brandy's exhilarated state.

Suddenly, no matter how appetizing the thought, she didn't want to be another frothy dessert on Griffen's menu. She wanted to be the entree, the main course, the principal dish, something so substantial and so satisfying that he would never desire a sweet again. Reality hit her! She had fallen in love with Griffen St. Clair!

Brandy rubbed the center of her throbbing forehead with three trembling fingers. Her main passion had always been her career. Why did this man have to come along and change that? Griffen didn't want love; he only wanted a body in bed. Her body—and why not? Hadn't she been giving the impression that every man in Florida had already had the same privilege!

"Here we are." Griffen's deep voice broke into the silent battle being waged in Brandy's mind.

She needed time. Her eyes sought the digital display on the dashboard. He was taking the midnight flight, he'd have to leave by eleven thirty. That left her just one hour—sixty minutes. She took a deep, controlling breath; she could handle that!

It was a cold sober, almost defiant Brandy Abbott that unlocked the cabin door and perversely punched

169

the overhead dinette light on. The austere glare was hardly conducive to romance and neither were the kitchen surroundings.

Brandy glanced pointedly to the cypress wall clock. "It looks like you'll just barely have enough time for coffee before you have to leave," she announced brightly. She tossed her purse onto the counter and quickly went to assemble the percolator that was lying in the drainboard. Brandy grinned smugly—coffee would be the perfect diversion.

Griffen smoothed his dark mustache. His hand hid a rather satanic smile; his dark eyes watched her flustered movements. "I was expecting something a little more potent."

She cast a cool, backward glance over her shoulder. "I'm afraid I don't have any liquor," she told him, being deliberately obtuse. Brandy was distressed to discover that Griffen had shed his jacket and tie, rolled up his sleeves, and unbuttoned his white silk shirt nearly to the waist. The mat of dark hair that curled against his bronze chest caused an inward flow of sensations that started in her stomach and curled downward. She hastily turned her attentions back to the coffeepot.

"I wasn't referring to alcohol." A deep voice growled in her ear; ten viselike fingers clamped around her waist. Brandy gasped as she was spun around and hauled roughly against Griffen's muscular physique. "Relax, darling." His hands moved up her back to her bare shoulders. He kneaded and massaged the tense, creamy skin.

"I . . . I'm quite relaxed, thank you," Brandy stammered. She tried to wedge her palms against his chest, but he shifted his position and she found her hands around his neck.

"I can feel just how taut and strained your body is." He smiled into her wide, blinking eyes. "It's all my fault, isn't it, Brandy? All this nervous frustration made you call for a man like Pierre."

Griffen lowered his head, his hot breath seared her cheek. "I don't want Pierre to have you. *I* want you." His lips formed each word against her mouth. "I want to feel your long sleek legs wrapped around my body. I want to taste and explore the deepest recesses of your desire."

"Griffen, stop! Please!" Brandy cried out in abject fear, making a valiant effort to twist free.

He laughed and propelled her backward onto the kitchen table. He was on top of her, his sinewy strength pinning her feverish, writhing body against the Formica surface. "What's one more man? One more night?" His deep voice growled. His hands tangled in the silken glory of her hair, imprisoning her head for his ruthless inspection.

"You don't understand," her trembling voice pleaded. Her moist eyes silently begged while her heart pounded furiously against the masculine chest that crushed her.

His hard mouth, compelling and purposeful, consumed her strangled protest. Griffen had meant to just scare her, to torture and tease, but suddenly he found himself out of control. He was starving for this amber-maned temptress, hungry for her kisses, ravenous for her lush body, anxious to devour her very soul!

His plundering tongue forced her lips apart,

thrusting deep into the moist sweetness of her mouth, thirsting to savor its pleasures. His urgent fingers deftly pushed aside the thin straps of her dress. He freed her breasts from their silky covering, teasing the swelling mounds until the urgent rosy peaks begged for attention.

Brandy's body vibrated under a turbulent force of unleashed primitive passion. An inexorable fever erupted in her blood. Her skin felt hot and tingling, shot through with delicious sensations. Her breasts throbbed beneath his caressing fingers. She moaned softly; her hands slid under his shirt, roaming over the working muscles of his back and shoulders, pressing into his heated flesh.

Griffen pulled his mouth free of her lips. His dark eyes glowed with naked desire. "Brandy, you are utterly delicious." His voice was hoarse, his breathing labored. His mustache nuzzled the sensitive skin at the base of her throat; his hands boldly pushed up the skirt of her dress.

Her fingers laced in the vibrant dark coils of hair at the nape of his neck, she pressed his head tightly against her breast, shivering as his warm lips and moist tongue played with the taut nipple.

Her damp body was pressed into the cold hardness of the table by the virile length of the man above. "You are so beautiful," Griffen whispered huskily. "I love the feel of you against me." His mouth was passionately persuasive when it tenderly conquered her half-parted lips. His bold finger shot forth and split her sheer panty hose. His hand smoothed the lean skin of her thigh before venturing higher, seeking the leg opening of her silken briefs.

The ripping sound penetrated her passion-drugged brain. Brandy's lashes fluttered open, her dilated pupils stared into the bright, gaudy ceiling fixture. The light was harsh and clinical. The room looked cheap and tawdry. Love turned into sex. And that wasn't what she wanted. She was overcome by a mixture of sorrow and anger.

Brandy froze, her body no longer obedient and yielding. "Stop it, Griffen!" Her voice was sharp and strong. Reality replaced desire with each passing second.

Griffen shook his dark head. "Brandy, what the—"

She took advantage of his confusion. Hands that had just caressed and held him now shoved him away. Clutching her dress, Brandy scrambled off the table and bolted for the bathroom, securely snapping the lock.

"Brandy!" Griffen's knuckles pounded against the door. "Come out of there. I want to talk to you!"

"No!" She shouted, hurriedly dragging the clothes hamper against the vibrating wooden frame. "I choose the man. I choose the night. And it's not you and it's not tonight!"

Griffen groaned and slammed his palms against the door. "Brandy, let me explain."

"Go away!" She yelled and turned on the shower, the sound of the water drowning out his words.

Griffen leaned against the wall, rubbing the back of his neck with his hands. He had certainly made a mess of things. The alarm on his gold watch played its musical reminder. He frowned and raised his hand once again against the solid bathroom door.

"Brandy," he shouted, raising his voice above the sound of rushing water, "we'll settle this when I get back."

Brandy sat on the closed cover of the commode and contemplated the beige floor tiles. The steam from the shower had left her limp and miserable and her head throbbed under a continual somersault of emotions.

She reached over, turned off the water, and listened. Cautiously she opened the door and peered out. The lights were on, but the room was empty. Brandy breathed a sigh of relief and flopped onto the sofa.

The sharp ring of the telephone made her jump. She anxiously looked at the wall clock. It couldn't be Griffen, he would be in the air by now.

Judy Durant's voice lilted in her ear. "Brandy? I've been trying to get you all night. Are you all right?"

"I'm just fine," she lied. "Is there some problem?"

"I was hoping you'd tell me."

Brandy frowned, her voice echoed her confusion. "I'm afraid I don't understand, Judy."

"Oh, dear. I'm probably putting my foot in my mouth, but I can't help it." A self-conscious laugh escaped her. "I know something was wrong today between you and Griffen. He reacted so strangely when he saw Pierre and then—"

"Pierre?" Brandy swallowed and straightened up against the sofa cushions. "You . . . you mean Griffen knows that Pierre is a porcelain bird?"

"Now you're doing it," Judy grumbled. "Of

course he's a bird. You ordered him!" She gave a long sigh. "Did you get the message that your brother called?"

Brandy closed her eyes and felt sick. "Griffen knows about Tony too," she whispered, her hands tightening on the telephone receiver.

"Then he did give you the message?"

"Yes, Judy, he certainly did."

By dawn Brandy had worn a path through the brown tweed carpet in the living room and stored enough precious gems of enmity to sustain her until Griffen returned to Florida.

So he had known all along about Pierre and he knew about Tony. So what was tonight? Her hands raked through her tumbled hair. Tonight was to be his revenge!

She wasn't stalemated—not yet. Brandy pulled out the chair by her design board and drafted a countermove. By noon she had completed her plans. With a little help from her friends, Griffen St. Clair would meet his match on Tuesday!

## CHAPTER TEN

Brandy was sitting on the corner of his desk completely engrossed in buffing her nails when Griffen arrived at nine o'clock Tuesday morning.

Her long legs were crossed at the knee, the slim cream-colored skirt hiked up to show a healthy expanse of sleek thigh. The taupe silk blouse was unbuttoned to a hazardous depth, revealing full, rounded, sun-toasted cleavage and urgent nipples that were highly visible beneath the slinky material.

The recessed fluorescent lights made her shoulder-length hair shimmer under a fluid of amber and gold waves. The subtle nuance of jasmine cologne lifted into the atmosphere and created an aura of pure seduction.

All in all it was the most provocative greeting he had ever encountered. Griffen's mouth twisted in wry amusement. He wondered what Brandy had in store for him now! "This is quite a homecoming."

She affected a healthy modicum of surprise, fluttering her mascara-ladened lashes and pursing her amber-glossed lips. "Welcome back," her throaty voice purred. She watched him toss his briefcase onto the upholstered client's chair and move to stand in front of her.

The nail buffer bounced silently to the carpet as Brandy wriggled off the edge of the desk and slid her soft, feminine curves against Griffen's athletic physique. "It seems like you've been away months instead of days." Her lips spoke in whispers against the corner of his mouth.

Griffen's long arms obediently wrapped themselves around her slender waist. "Is this the same woman I left locked in a bathroom on Friday?" came his dry rejoinder.

She gave a musical sigh of concern and her diamond eyes widened innocently. "I'm really so ashamed and embarrassed." Her fingers smoothed the lapels of his charcoal suit and moved to play with the buttons of his blue shirt. "I've spent the last few days trying to understand why that happened."

"And have you?" His brown eyes narrowed inquiringly while his hands freely roamed over her silk-covered back and shoulders.

Brandy nodded and burrowed closer. Her pelvis and breasts burned their womanly imprint into his masculine attire. "You had become almost a religious figure to me." Her lashes lowered demurely to study the intricate swirl pattern of his tie. "I know how anxious you . . . are . . . to reform me, but Griffen—" she gave another little sigh, her lips nuz-

177

zled his freshly shaven jaw "—I don't think that's possible."

"I see," he muttered, but he didn't and right at this moment Griffen couldn't have cared less. He was too busy caressing the erogenous terrain of her sensuous body.

"Tonight—" Brandy's throaty voice vibrated in his ear "—tonight I want to make amends. I want you to have what you so richly deserve."

Her even white teeth nipped his ear lobe as her fingers snaked through the dark coils of hair on the back of his head. "I've planned an evening you'll never forget in a place that will satisfy your every fantasy and fulfill your every desire."

Brandy looked at him; the black pupils of her eyes dominated the smoky-blue irises. "Believe me, darling, tonight you'll be very pleased." Her half-parted lips enticed his mouth, but just as they connected, the intercom interrupted obscenely.

"That's all right." She squeezed his well-muscled forearm. "I'm afraid I have an appointment and I'm already late."

Griffen stared in fascination at the provocative rhythm of her hips beneath the clingy skirt as she glided from his office. It took four rather rude blasts from the intercom to jar him from his erotic musings. He shook his head, undraped his tie from his ear, and lifted the phone receiver.

It was after two when Brandy returned to her office, her appointments had run long and the fast-food hamburger she had consumed over ten traffic lights was aggravating her digestive tract. Despite all

178

that, she felt deliciously exhilarated about the evening ahead. "Where is our illustrious employer?" She grinned at Judy Durant. "Still out to lunch?"

The petite redhead shook her head and snapped off her electric typewriter. "He went out to the airport to pick up his mother; she arrived a day early."

Brandy pursed her lips and frowned, wondering if this new development would force her to cancel her plans. "How long is she visiting?"

Judy handed Brandy a stack of mail. "Oh, she's not visiting. Now that the condo is finished, she'll be moving in. I bet she's going to love the penthouse."

Letters and pamphlets fell from Brandy's leaden fingers and scattered all over the reception desk. "The . . . the penthouse?" She swallowed and cleared her throat. "I . . . I thought the penthouse was for Griffen."

"No, it's to replace the house Mrs. St. Clair lost during last year's hurricane." Judy eyed Brandy's pale features curiously.

"What are you so worried about? I saw the penthouse Friday morning. It looked beautiful."

"That . . . that was before I made some changes," she stammered. Her shoulders sagged. "What time will Griffen be back?"

"He's not coming back. In fact he should be showing his mother through the Shoals just about now."

A horrified gasp escaped Brandy. She grabbed her purse and darted out the front door, leaving Judy sputtering in surprise.

The fifteen-minute drive to the condo dragged on for what seemed like hours. Brandy prayed the traffic would speed up, the plane would be late, the elevator in the Shoals would break down, or the earth would open and swallow her and the van. None of her prayers were answered.

She barged into the penthouse, her clothes sticking to her perspiration-soaked body, her chest heaving under convulsive breathing. Wild, distraught eyes noted the door of the master bedroom was still closed. Her ears registered the sound of voices drifting in from the roof garden.

Brandy took a deep breath. All she had to do was keep Griffen and his mother out of that bedroom. She crossed her fingers and hoped a burst of clever creativity would flood her mind.

But it was Griffen's voice that invaded her thoughts. "Well, this is a nice surprise."

A tremulous laugh escaped Brandy's lips. "My goodness, I didn't expect to find anyone." Her tongue moistened her dry lips. "I was going to work in here today."

He shook his dark head and stared at her. "I can't imagine what you have left to do. The place is finished right down to the cakes of soap in the bathroom."

"Griffen." She laughed again, her shaky fingers rubbing the strain from the back of her neck. "What might appear finished to you is still unfinished to me. I'm afraid that I'm rather like those temperamental artists who hate having people peek at the canvases before the official unveiling."

A slim, dark-haired woman in a white blouse and slacks entered from the sliding glass doors. "I am in love with that darling pelican, what did you say his

180

name was? I—" she stopped and looked questioningly at the new arrival.

"Mother." Griffen slid his arm around Brandy's waist and guided her toward the older woman. "This is Brandy Abbott."

"It's a pleasure to meet you, Mrs. St. Clair." Brandy smiled politely and extended her hand.

"My dear, I have been hearing about you all weekend." Mrs. St. Clair clasped Brandy's outstretched hand warmly. "Griffen—" her eyes darted to her son's smiling face "—you're right, she is lovely."

"Thank . . . thank you," Brandy stammered uncomfortably, trying to control the flood of color that tinged her cheeks. "I really must apologize for the condition of the penthouse."

"Apologize?" Mrs. St. Clair echoed, her blue eyes widening in surprise. "My dear, it's a work of art." Her jeweled hand swept over the elegantly furnished living room. The neutral-toned conversation group and natural textures of a bamboo coffee table, durrie rug, and wall decorations balanced an array of Oriental art objects.

"Brandy," Griffen chided, his fingers squeezing her waist, "whatever has gotten into you?"

She smiled at Mrs. St. Clair, took a deep breath, and turned the force of her stormy blue eyes on Griffen. "You never told me that this place was for your mother." Her words inched out through clenched teeth.

He shrugged his broad shoulders. "What's the problem? She loves it."

Brandy turned her head, noting with satisfaction that his mother was inspecting the Chinese wall mural in the Georgian dining room. She swallowed and eyed him hesitantly. "I thought this place was yours." She cleared her throat and lowered her lashes. "I . . . I made some last-minute changes for tonight."

"Tonight?" He looked confused then grinned. "Oh, that little scene you played this morning." Griffen's thumb and forefinger grasped Brandy's chin. He smiled tenderly into her anxious features. "Darling, I think it's time that we both stopped all of this nonsense. I've known the truth about you since Friday." His long fingers caressed the curve of her jaw before tangling in the soft waves of her hair. "I will admit my revenge got a little out of hand."

"Oh, Griffen." She closed her eyes and took a deep breath. "I knew you knew, that's why I was acting so outrageous this morning." Brandy's palms slapped against his broad chest. "You weren't supposed to happen!"

"What wasn't supposed to happen, Brandy?" he demanded. His eyes darkened and his voice deepened.

"Falling in love with you." She could have sworn she said those words only in her mind. But then she was jerked roughly into his arms. His warm, wonderful mouth closed tenderly over her trembling lips.

Brandy wound her arms tightly around his neck. Her body arched in a silent, sinuous invitation against him while her lips and tongue returned his passion with matched desire.

"It really isn't fair, Griffen." She rested her forehead against his. "You've been absolutely horrible to

182

me from the very beginning," Brandy reminded him in a breathless voice.

"I guess I do have a lot to make up for," he murmured huskily. His knuckles gently caressed the nape of her neck. "I love you very much. You have haunted me night and day since we met." His mouth twisted in a humorless grin. "I used to think people who said things like that were foolish, but now I know different."

She laughed delightedly; her eyes sparkled into his. "I knew something was the matter when I dreamed about you instead of concrete and steel." The soft pads of her fingers lovingly pressed along the curve of his cheek to the dark hairs of his mustache.

His teeth lightly nipped her fingertips. "I must admit marriage to you will give me the maximum temptation and the maximum opportunity for indulgence."

"Marriage?" She suddenly became very serious. "I didn't think you'd want to get married."

"What did you think I wanted?" Griffen asked in a cold, brittle tone. A mask slid over his face; his dark eyes narrowed. "Or wouldn't you consider marrying a divorced man?"

The singularly sweet kiss Brandy placed on a corner of his mouth sought to dispel his fears. "That has nothing to do with it." Her lips curved into a gentle smile; her fingertips stroked away the harsh lines that were etched on his lean features.

"I was thinking about you, Griffen. You deserve a woman who will have only you in her life, someone who'll have dinner on the table, keep an impeccable house, and won't be too exhausted when you want to make love."

Her luminous gaze searched his face. "My life won't be my own for quite a while. I don't want to be burdened with a house to run, dinners to prepare, and children, at least not for a few years." Brandy took a deep breath. "As much as I love you, I won't give up my career. I'll live with you as long as you'd like."

He cradled her face in his large hands. "I don't expect you to give up the things you love for me." Griffen smiled tenderly into her anxious features. "I won't mind sharing you, I won't mind eating a dinner of corn flakes, and I won't mind just holding you at night." He kissed the tip of her nose then each eyelid. "I'm not marrying you just to have a combination mistress and maid. From the very beginning I loved your strength, your talent, your energy. I want to share your achievements and your failures. I want you and I want it legal—you deserve nothing less than that." His arms wrapped around her in the most reassuring manner. He pressed her head against his heart.

The throbbing refrain from Ravel's Bolero pulsated into the living room. Brandy gave a horrified gasp. "Oh, my God, your mother!" She bolted from Griffen's embrace and ran to the doorway. A rather dazed Mrs. St. Clair stumbled out of the bedroom.

"Are you all right?" Brandy helped her future mother-in-law to a nearby lacquered, cushioned side chair.

Mrs. St. Clair blinked and cleared her throat. "That certainly is an interesting room." She took a

184

deep breath and smoothed a stray wisp of dark hair into the fold of her chignon. "It just took me by surprise."

Griffen's bellow replaced Ravel's. Brandy winced; a low moan escaped her throat.

Mrs. St. Clair smiled and patted her hand. "Why don't I walk to that darling little shopping mall in the next block." She stood up and neatened the collection of gold chains around her slender throat. "I can spend hours in a boutique." Her finely plucked brow arched expressively when her son emitted another roar. "I'll take a cab back to the office later."

"What would you call this masterpiece?" Griffen inquired in a dry tone, still blinking in amazement when Brandy wandered in to survey her handiwork.

The bedroom was a medley of reflective achievement. Mirrored panels concealed the closets, closed off the windows, and lined the ceiling. The occupants of the room were repeated in sensorial infinity.

The diaphanous draperies that tumbled from a high wooden frame over the king-size waterbed seemed wafted by an ocean breeze. Recessed lights under the bed and a large aquarium in the opposite wall reflected their shimmering images around the room. The illusion was one of being adrift in a goldfish bowl.

"It's my own design." Brandy cast a humorous sidelong glance at Griffen. "I call it Early Lust."

"And all of this was for tonight?"

She nodded and bent to smooth the white satin bedsheet. "I did promise you a fantasy."

Griffen walked over and stood in front of her. "You are awfully good at being bad."

Brandy looked at him, her eyes wide and luminous. "Do you really think so?" Her smooth forehead puckered thoughtfully. "With most men I'm a frigid fish, a frozen entree, but with you . . . it was spontaneous combustion."

He laughed and slid his arms around her waist. "And just what were your plans tonight?" He studied the rounded contours of her upturned face; his eyes flared alive.

"To follow my baser instincts." Brandy's hands slid beneath the shoulders of his jacket and tugged it free of his muscular torso. She quickly disposed of his tie and unbuttoned his shirt. Her fingers tumbled over the buckle on his wide leather belt, finally unhooked it, then boldly sought the zipper. Griffen kicked his pants aside and removed his shoes, socks, and briefs.

"I was planning to torment and tease." Her voice was low and urgent, her eyes locked into his. "But I'm afraid I can't." She unbuttoned her blouse, stepped out of her skirt and petticoat. Shoes, panty hose, and panties drifted on top of the pile of masculine clothing that littered the white shag carpet.

Brandy came to him, the friction of silken skin sliding against hair-roughened flesh igniting a tongue of fire that enflamed them both. Her tongue outlined his firm, masculine lips, then teasingly darted into his mouth. Her fingers ruffled the dark hair at his sideburns and moved down the nape of his neck to lightly scratch a circular pattern across the curve of his shoulders.

Griffen gave a low groan and took control. His kisses were more savage than gentle, ravishing her soft lips and branding his ownership on her eager mouth. His hands glided over her supple spine and curved around her firm buttocks. He pressed her tightly against him, his male hardness prodded her insistently, leaving Brandy in no doubt of the extent of his arousal.

He guided her backward onto the waterbed. Her pliant form dissolved into the mattress; the undulating movements of the waves lifted her against his virile length.

His hand outlined the lush curves and angles of her body. "You are exquisite," he breathed. His hands cupped and lifted her breasts, his tongue and teeth teasing and nibbling the hardened peaks. His lips blazed a fiery trail across her flat stomach, the hairs of his mustache tickled her navel, his fingers slid between her long legs and parted her thighs.

She moaned softly as he bathed her with the warm dampness of his mouth. The sensuous torment of his gently probing finger created sensations she had never before experienced.

Brandy pulled his head back to hers. "I love you." The ache in her voice echoed the frenzy of erotic sensations that tormented her skin. Their lips and tongues continued their languorous explorations while their hands and fingers explored the inherent differences between the sexes.

Suddenly Griffen hovered over her face. He lifted her hips to meet his thrusting desire. His maleness filled the core of her femininity. Two singulars became plural in complete and utter emotional, mental, and physical fusion. This was no one-sided possession, but a joyful union of love that completed them both.

Her long legs wrapped around his powerful hips, she felt him move inside of her, the force of him growing stronger and deeper. Griffen knew when to be tender and when to be rough. It was an exhilarating experience. A crescendo of sensual pleasure ignited the primitive passion that lay hidden in her soul. Her body vibrated around him, her own rhythmic movements synchronized with his.

The inward flow of sensations were building out of control. Her passion erupted in a nerve-shattering explosion. Her teeth sank into Griffen's shoulder.

He pulled her closer, his body shuddering and trembling under the violence of his climax. Griffen rolled over and took Brandy with him, their sweat-anointed, love-replete bodies still fused together.

They were both breathless; their hearts pounded in unison, echoing the intensity of their splended arousal. Griffen placed a gossamer kiss on a corner of her mouth; his eyes worshiped her every feature. "I love you so very much," he vowed in a reverent, husky voice.

Brandy snuggled against his heated flesh. She felt content, relaxed, and secure. "Griffen—" she stirred lazily, studying him through her lashes "—if this penthouse is for your mother, where do you live?"

He grinned at her, his hands settling on the curve of her spine. "There's an apartment over the office, but that will never do now. I think we can come to a compromise with my mother; she was very fond of the Oriental three-bedroom model you did."

"Lovely, because I am very fond of this place and

this room." Her hands slid between their entwined bodies to the spot where they were still joined together, she felt him hardening again. "Griffen . . ."

He grinned, his dark eyes intrigued with the reflections in the mirrors. "I just want to disprove that health bulletin about smoking and impotence."

*LOOK FOR NEXT MONTHS*
*CANDLELIGHT ECSTASY ROMANCES*™: